The Money Hunt

Frank grabbed a stick and carefully stirred through the branches on the trail floor. One by one they fell off the pile until Frank could see the object buried underneath.

The steely jaws of a heavy metal bear trap gaped at him.

Frank's stomach did a flipflop as he stared at the deadly trap. He took a deep breath and let it out slowly. "I'd better find Joe," he murmured.

Frank turned around to backtrack—and nearly leapt back into the jaws of the trap behind him.

A huge, dark form was blocking the trail Frank had used. The older Hardy brother froze to the spot.

He was face to face with an uncaged, untamed, and hungry-looking bear!

The Hardy Boys Mystery Stories

Available from MINSTREL Books

THE MONEY HUNT

FRANKLIN W. DIXON

PUBLISHED BY POCKET BOOKS

New York   London   Toronto   Sydney   Tokyo   Singapore

A MINSTREL PAPERBACK *ORIGINAL*

 A Minstrel Book published by
POCKET BOOKS, a division of Simon & Schuster Inc.
1230 Avenue of the Americas, New York, NY 10020

ISBN: 0-671-69451-0

First Minstrel Books printing April 1990

10 9 8 7 6 5 4 3 2 1

Contents

THE MONEY
HUNT

1 A Change of Plan

"This vacation is going to be *great*," said seventeen-year-old Joe Hardy. He unfolded a road map of the eastern United States and spread it out on the kitchen table. He bent his blond head over the table and ran his finger along the turnpike on the map. "And if we take this route, we can make it to Florida in two days, tops," he added.

Joe's eighteen-year-old brother, Frank, looked down at the map. "Yeah, but all we'll see on the trip is highway," he said. "I think the shore route would be less boring."

The Hardys were getting ready to drive south with their friends Chet Morton and Biff Hooper for a fall vacation.

"But the highway is faster," protested Joe. "The

1

four of us decided we wanted some intense Florida sun, sand, and surf, remember?"

Frank ran his fingers through his dark brown hair as he studied the map more closely.

"Well, then why don't we split it?" he suggested. He began to trace different roads on the map with his forefinger. "Part of the time we'll stick to the turnpikes and highways. Part of the time we'll take smaller roads through interesting places."

Joe shook his head. "Get real, Frank. If we take *your* route, we'll be on the road until Christmas. Now, *my* way is the fastest and easiest, no doubt about it."

"Where's your sense of adventure?" Frank asked. "I mean, where would Columbus have gotten if he'd stuck to a map?"

Joe rolled his blue eyes. "Right. Sure. But here's the key showing the mileage and—"

"Look," Frank interrupted. "This is getting us nowhere." He thought for a moment. Then his brown eyes lit up, and he said, "Tell you what, why don't we go talk to Dad and see what he says?"

"Fine by me," Joe agreed, folding up the map.

They headed upstairs to their parents' bedroom. The door was closed.

"What if he's asleep?" Joe asked. "He's been taking a lot of naps since the accident."

Frank and Joe's father, Fenton Hardy, was a

former New York City police officer turned private investigator. He'd become injured a few nights earlier while tailing a suspect. Fenton lost the suspect and had taken himself off the case when he tripped over a flower pot and severely sprained his ankle. The doctor had told him to get plenty of bed rest. Fenton was doing his best to follow the doctor's orders.

"I can't believe Dad told us, Mom, and Aunt Gertrude not to put off our vacations," Joe said.

"Well, he can get around okay on his crutches," Frank replied. He smiled. "And anyway, he's probably fed up with the fuss we've all been making over him." He tapped lightly on the bedroom door, then called out softly, "Dad. Are you awake?"

The brothers heard a muffled voice say, "Come in."

Frank opened the door. He and Joe stepped into the room.

Fenton was sitting on the bed propped up against two pillows. A mystery novel lay facedown and open on his chest. His bandaged ankle was resting on another pillow.

"What's up?" Fenton asked, smiling at his sons.

"Dad, we have a problem," Joe announced as the brothers moved toward the bed. "We can't decide on the best way to drive to Florida and—"

Before Joe could finish his sentence, the bedside phone began to ring.

Lifting the receiver, Fenton gestured for them to wait.

"Yes, this is Fenton Hardy. Who? Steve? Steve Johnson?" Fenton grinned. "Well, what do you know! After all these years! What are you up to these days? You are? That's great. Sure, I'm still in the private eye business. You what? That sounds serious, Steve. Look, I'd do it in a minute, but I'm afraid I can't. I sprained my ankle pretty badly. All in the line of duty. It's a long story. . . . Suppose I send my boys? Right, Frank and Joe. They'll be happy to investigate the situation for you."

When the brothers heard the word "investigate" and their names mentioned, they looked at each other, then at their father.

"Let me write this down," said Fenton, reaching for a pencil and notepad next to the telephone. There was a long silence while he wrote. Finally he said, "Okay, near the dock—right. What time will it leave? Uh-huh, uh-huh, right. I have it. Stop worrying, Steve, everything will be all right. So long."

"Sounds like our services were volunteered," said Frank as soon as Fenton put down the receiver.

"Sounds like our vacation was cancelled," said Joe.

"I hope you two won't mind helping out an old friend of mine," said Fenton. "He owns a hunting

4

lodge in the Maine woods, and it sounds as though he's in some trouble."

"What kind of trouble, Dad?" asked Frank.

"Yeah," said Joe. "And who is Steve Johnson anyway?"

Fenton smiled. "Steve and I were at the police academy together. He and I served in the same precinct, but he left the force several years before I did, and we lost touch. A few years ago, he bought and renovated a run-down hunting lodge in northern Maine—Lakeside Lodge. The lodge has been doing very well since he took it over."

"Then what's his problem?" asked Joe.

"Something strange is going on up there," Fenton replied, frowning. "Guests almost getting caught in illegally set animal traps. People hearing a chainsaw buzzing in the middle of the night."

Frank gave a low whistle. "That definitely sounds weird. And those traps are dangerous."

Fenton nodded. "Steve's afraid word may get out that the lodge is dangerous. That could undo all his hard work." Fenton paused for a moment.

"There's something else, isn't there, Dad?" said Frank. "Let's have it."

Fenton gave his sons a half-smile. "You're not going to believe this, but some guests have reported seeing a ghost," he said.

"A ghost?" said Joe. "Let's get real, Dad."

5

"I know, I know." Fenton raised his hand. "But the guests have obviously seen *something* strange. Put that together with all the other happenings, and it's enough to worry Steve a lot."

"A haunted hunting lodge—that's the kind of reputation that could definitely keep guests away," said Frank. "Not exactly the peace and quiet they'd expect."

"Peace and quiet are just what people look for up there. Lakeside Lodge is really deep in those Maine woods. So deep you can only get there by a seaplane that lands near it on the lake."

"You mean there are no roads?" Joe said.

"Well, there are old logging roads. They wander through more than twenty miles of forest that was once owned by a big paper company. It would be a pretty winding, bumpy ride." Fenton sighed. "Maine. I'd leap at the chance to wander through those 'murmuring pines and the hemlocks,' as the poet says."

"You're not leaping or wandering anywhere for a while, Dad," Frank observed. He looked at Joe. "So I guess this is our case."

"Right. We can always hit the Florida trail in the spring," Joe added.

"Sure," Frank said, smiling. "Why should we hurry just to lie on a beach under the blazing sun when we can spend time investigating a ghost in the subzero warmth of northern Maine?"

6

"Boogie with a bear!" Joe said with a grin.

"Really get to know our friend, the moose," said Frank. He and his brother burst out laughing.

"All right, you two," Fenton said. "Let's get serious. If someone is deliberately making trouble, there could be real danger. Now pay attention. We've arranged for you to leave tomorrow morning. Here's how you'll get to Lakeside Lodge. . . ."

"Too bad Chet and Biff couldn't come with us," Joe commented as he peered out the seaplane's window. "Maine is really beautiful."

It was midafternoon the next day. The Hardy brothers had taken an early plane for Portland, Maine. At the Portland airport, they'd booked a flight on a four-seater seaplane piloted by Captain Jerry Barnes. Frank and Joe were the only passengers. The plane was also carrying supplies for Steve Johnson.

They were flying north, high above a landscape thick with fir trees and dotted with small lakes.

Captain Barnes turned his head toward the brothers. "I'm glad you like the Pine Tree State," he said, smiling.

"How close are we to Lakeside Lodge, Captain Barnes?" Frank asked.

"Call me Jerry," said the captain. "Everyone else does." He pointed to a body of water below them. "That's Moosehead Lake. Mirror Lake, the lake the

7

lodge is on, is about ten miles north of Moosehead Lake. We should be there in about twenty minutes."

Leaning forward, Joe stared out the window at the sparkling water. "Wow, I never knew there was a lake this big in New England."

Frank grinned. "Well, we all know geography's not your strong point."

"Give me a break," Joe said. "I know what the capitol of Maine is, anyway."

"Big deal," Frank said. "Everyone *knows* it's Portland."

Joe shook his head and grinned. "Wrong. It's Augusta."

"He's right, Frank," they heard Jerry Barnes say.

"Okay, okay," Frank said, holding up his hands. "I guess I need to brush up on my geography, too."

About fifteen minutes later, Jerry Barnes said, "You two had better fasten your seat belts. We're approaching Mirror Lake, and I'm going to start our descent."

Frank and Joe buckled their seat belts as the plane began to lose altitude.

"See that cluster of buildings straight ahead?" Jerry asked. "That's all part of Lakeside Lodge. That big old house is the main lodge."

"That must be the dock where we'll land," Frank said.

"Where?" asked Joe, squinting.

"Follow along the shore to the right," his brother replied. "Around that bend, then the little sandy beach. Then see that shack and the dock sticking out?" Frank asked.

"I see it. And it's getting closer," said Joe. He tightened his seat belt. "Well, get ready for 'splashdown.'"

Jerry released the landing gear, then the pontoon floats. He cut the engine as the plane glided lower and lower over the lake.

Finally the plane came to a stop about a foot from the dock. It bobbed up and down a bit in the water.

"I can't believe what a smooth landing that was," Joe said, as he and Frank unbuckled their seat belts.

"What were you expecting?" asked Frank. "A tidal wave?"

"Actually, some of my landings have been pretty bumpy in bad weather," Jerry said. He had climbed into the passenger area and was opening the door.

Frank and Joe stepped out of the plane onto the dock. Standing in front of them was a tall, dark-haired man in a red-checked jacket.

"Looks like Jerry delivers the goods once again," said the tall man. He held out his hand. "I'm Steve Johnson. You must be Frank and Joe."

"That's us," Frank said, nodding. He and Joe shook hands with Steve Johnson. "Dad sends his best regards."

"And his best designated hitters," Steve said with

a smile. Then, as Jerry Barnes unloaded several cartons filled with supplies and mail, he added, "I sure hope you guys can help figure out what's going on here." He shook his head. "I guess Fenton told you about the near-accidents with the traps and the chainsaw—and our 'ghost.'"

"He mentioned them," Joe said. "But we need to get your version of the story."

"Let's get back to the lodge first," Steve suggested. "Here, we can stow your stuff in the back of the truck." He led the way to a dark red pickup truck parked at the end of the dock.

Steve and the Hardys helped Jerry load the cartons into the truck. Then they thanked him for the ride.

After the plane took off, Steve said, "Hop in. The engine may be a little cold. The truck's been standing here since yesterday. Willy, my caretaker, got a flat and came back this morning to fix it. He just dropped me off in the small jeep. I figured I'd need room for your gear plus the supplies."

"Oh, we travel light," Joe said, climbing in beside Frank.

"You'd be surprised how much baggage some of these hunters from the city bring up," Steve said, shaking his head. "You'd think they were going to be away for a year instead of a week or two."

After several tries, the truck's engine roared to

life. Steve headed the truck down a winding dirt road filled with ruts.

"I . . . can see . . . why a seaplane is the best . . . way to . . . get here," Joe said breathlessly. "This road's pretty bumpy!"

Steve grinned. "The road will smooth out soon."

He was right. A few minutes later, the road became much smoother. Frank and Joe settled back in their seats and began to enjoy the sight of the thick pine forest and needle-covered ground on either side of the road.

"We're almost there," Steve said. "It's just around this bend and then downhill about a quarter of a mile."

They started down the hill. As they did, the truck began to pick up speed.

"There's the main lodge ahead," Frank said, pointing to a large, two-story log building. "Hey, aren't we going a little fast?"

Joe sucked in his breath. "We're going to drive right through the lodge at this rate."

"Put on the brakes, Steve!" Frank shouted.

The older man looked at them, his eyes filled with fear. "I am! The pedal's hitting the floor . . . but nothing's happening. We have no brakes!"

2 Cabin Fever

The truck sped down the hill, faster and faster.

Steve slammed his foot down on the clutch pedal. It didn't stop the careening pickup, but it did take them out of gear.

At the same time, Frank grabbed the gearshift and yanked it into low gear. Steve let up on the clutch pedal. The truck screeched as it began slowing down.

The abrupt change of gears threw the vehicle into a skid. Finally it swerved to a halt at a ninety-degree angle to the road—right in front of the lodge.

The three of them sat in the cab, slightly dazed by the wild ride.

Suddenly they heard the sound of clapping.

Frank and Joe looked toward the porch. A white-haired man who looked to be in his sixties stood there, clapping his hands and grinning.

"That was some driving trick," he called out. "Trying to impress the guests, Steve?"

Steve leapt out of the truck, his face red with anger. "Willy, I thought you said the only problem with this truck was a flat tire!"

The white-haired man stared at Steve. "That's all that *was* wrong with it," he said.

"No, it's not." Steve's voice was still angry. "We nearly got killed just now, coming down the hill. The brakes gave out!"

Frowning, Willy came over and glanced around the pickup. "The brakes were fine when I drove the pickup yesterday," he assured Steve. "Otherwise, I'd have ended up in the lake. Couldn't say if anyone's been near it since." He shrugged. "I can't keep track of everything around here."

"Let's get the pickup around back and take a look at those brakes," said Steve.

Together Frank, Joe, and the two men pushed the pickup around the lodge to a shed behind the lodge, where Willy had set up a maintenance area.

Willy opened the hood of the pickup and looked inside. Then he slid under the truck. Several moments later he emerged from under the pickup. He stood up and wiped his greasy hands on a rag.

"Well?" Steve demanded impatiently. "What's wrong with the brakes?"

13

Willy shook his head. "It's unbelievable. Somebody got in there and removed the brake lining. And whoever did it knew exactly what he was doing."

The Hardys looked at Steve. He had a worried look on his face.

"Let's keep this to ourselves, okay?" Steve said to Willy. "We don't want to upset the guests."

"I'd like to get my hands on whoever's pulling these practical jokes," Willy muttered as he headed into the maintenance shed to get some tools to repair the damage.

Steve turned to Frank and Joe. "Another 'accident,'" he said. "We could have been killed. If the guests hear about this, they'll probably want to leave." Steve shook his head. "And I'm not sure I'd blame them."

"Look," Frank said. "Why don't we get settled in. Then you can tell us exactly what's been happening here."

"Fine," Steve said with a nod. "But how about some hot cocoa first? You guys look like you could use it."

"I wouldn't mind something," Joe said, flexing his gloved hands. He shivered slightly. "It seems a lot colder now than it did when we first got here."

"That's because the sun is going down," Frank said.

"Hey, this is tropical." Steve smiled at the Hardys. "The lake hasn't even started to freeze over yet." He stepped to the door of the maintenance shack. "Willy, we'll see you later. Would you drop off Frank and Joe's bags at cabin seven? Thanks."

Steve led Frank and Joe up the porch steps and into the lodge. They passed through a large but cozy-looking living room. The floor was covered with rugs and sofas, and comfortable-looking chairs were placed around the room. The walls were covered with paintings of wildlife and wilderness scenes. On one wall was a gigantic moose head. At one end of the room was a large flagstone fireplace. Inside the fireplace a fire crackled and hissed.

Frank and Joe sat at one end of the long pine trestle table in the lodge's dining room. Steve disappeared into the kitchen. Moments later he returned with three cups of steaming hot cocoa.

"First let me tell you something about the lodge's past," Steve said. "It has a history."

Joe took a sip of cocoa. "What kind of a history?"

"Thirteen years ago there was a big bank robbery down in Boston," Steve told the Hardys. "The guys who pulled it off got away and drove north, heading through Maine for Canada with the stolen money.

"There was a blizzard, and they got lost off the main roads. They ended up in this area. The barrier was down on one of the company's old roads

15

through the forest. They got on the road, and before the drifts got too high, they made their way here."

Steve shrugged. "Of course, the lodge was closed for the winter, but they broke in and holed up until the weather cleared. After a few weeks, they made a break for it, and a highway patrol chopper spotted them on one of the logging roads. Three of the robbers were caught, the fourth took off into the tall timber—and was never seen again."

Joe shuddered. "He must have frozen to death. What about the money?"

"The three robbers who were caught didn't have the loot. They said that the fourth guy had hidden it." Steve shook his head. "That left the lodge real popular with fortune hunters. They dug up the property and searched in the woods, but no one managed to find the money. The lodge's popularity lasted for about one season. Then business dropped like a stone. The owner got discouraged and let the lodge get run-down."

Moodily, Steve stirred his spoon around in his cup of cocoa. "It was always my dream to own a place like this. I've worked hard to make this place attractive and comfortable. I made it popular with hunters and vacationers again. That's why these 'accidents' are so hard to take."

"Tell us more about them," Frank suggested, leaning forward.

16

"What about the chainsaw you said you heard?" asked Joe. "That sounds really weird."

"It *is* weird," Steve said. "In the middle of the night, everyone will hear a chainsaw buzzing away somewhere in the woods. But there can't be anybody out there, because, as far as I know, everyone's here in bed." He sighed. "And I don't feel I can come right out and ask the guests if one of them is prowling around at night."

"How about neighbors?" Frank asked. "Are there any other camps nearby?"

"We're it between the north rim of Moosehead Lake and practically the Canadian border. We have Mirror Lake out front, and then we're surrounded by a thousand acres of the paper company's timberland. There's no way to get in here except by seaplane or helicopter. Unless, of course, you feel like slogging it over twenty miles of old logging road through the tall timber. The road's been closed for months now, anyway—even the paper company doesn't use it anymore. Jerry brings supplies to us twice a week."

He shook his head. "We've had a couple of good storms already. If you wanted to travel by road you'd have to use a bulldozer to get through on it. Most of it is covered with fallen trees by now."

"So it sounds as if the only possible suspects are the people here in the lodge," Frank said. "Unless

17

someone you don't know about is camping in the area."

"So far we've just got a mysterious chainsaw. What about those animal traps?" Joe asked.

"That was pretty scary," Steve replied. "Someone set two of those jaw-type traps in the woods. They're illegal because they're cruel to animals. A few of my guests almost got caught in them. The traps were covered by leaves and pine needles."

"Those traps can really injure humans, too," Frank said. "That's another reason they were banned."

"But that's not all," Steve continued. "There's more. We've had all kinds of things disappear, like tools. You know, a shovel here, an ax there. Not just lost or misplaced—vanished."

"Anything else?" asked Frank. "The, uh, ghost, for instance?"

"Oh, right," said Steve, looking a little embarrassed. "I know it sounds stupid, but the guests claim they see a ghost."

Frank and Joe looked at him in disbelief.

Steve held up his hands. "Yeah, I know. But everybody says the same thing. An eerie-looking figure dressed all in white comes roaring past the cabins and the lodge early in the morning, before breakfast. Some people have seen the ghost at dusk, too."

18

"What do you mean by 'roaring past'?" Frank asked.

Steve looked even more embarrassed. "Uh . . . the ghost drives past in our all-terrain vehicle."

"A ghost who can drive," Frank said. "That's a new one."

"Have you ever seen it, Steve?" Joe asked.

"No, but I hear the motor roaring through here when it whizzes by," Steve replied.

Joe turned to his brother. "What do you think is going on here? Got any ideas?"

Frank shook his head. "So far it sounds like someone's playing games. But they're dangerous games," he said. "Those brakes and those animal traps weren't rigged by a ghost."

"I can't figure out why anyone would want to 'get' me or ruin the lodge's reputation," Steve said. "Nobody's offered to buy the place or anything like that."

"We'll get to work on it first thing tomorrow morning," Frank promised.

"Right," Joe added. "Maybe we'll see our friend in the ATV."

"But now I think we should get settled in," Frank added.

"Fine." Steve smiled. "You're in cabin number seven. Just take a left when you walk out of the lodge. You shouldn't have trouble finding it, even

19

though all the cabins are surrounded by trees and bushes for privacy. They have numbers on little posts along the path. Oh, and by the way, dinner's at six-thirty."

"Great," Frank said. "We'll unpack, then take a little look around till dinnertime."

"When you come back here, I'll introduce you to everyone," Steve said.

"Just as friends," warned Joe. "We don't want anyone to know we're up here to investigate."

"What about hunting?" Steve asked.

"We don't have licenses, and we're not really interested anyway," said Frank. He thought for a moment. Then he said, "Look, why don't you introduce us as friends who are up here to write a story about Maine for our school paper."

"Good idea," Joe said approvingly. "I even brought my camera, so I'll be your photographer."

"Sounds good," Steve said with a smile. "Well, I'd better get back to lodge business. One of the guests wants to go fishing tomorrow, and I said I'd supply him with some tackle. I'll see you later."

"Okay," Frank said. "And don't worry, Steve," he added with a grin. "The Hardy brothers are the best ghost hunters around."

The Hardys left the lodge and walked along a dirt path that led to the cabins. A cluster of thick pines formed a dense row to one side. Short stakes with reflective numbers marked breaks in the wall of evergreens and indicated smaller paths that led to each cabin.

The Hardys found the stake marked with the number seven and turned off the main path.

The cabin was a small log building with two made-up beds, two armchairs, a closet, and a bathroom. A single window looked out onto the forest.

"So, what do we do first?" Joe asked as they entered the cabin.

"First we unpack, and then— What's that?" Frank lowered his voice suddenly.

"What?" asked Joe. "I don't hear anything."

"Shh!"

Then Joe heard it—a scratching sound that came from above their heads.

"Mice? Squirrels nesting up there?" Joe whispered.

"Maybe," Frank whispered back. "I'm going to investigate."

Frank took a quick look around the cabin. In the closet, he spotted an open trapdoor, which looked as if it led to a small attic.

"I'll give you a boost," Joe whispered. He clasped two hands under his brother's hiking boot and gave a slight heave.

Frank clutched the edge of the trapdoor, then raised himself up.

Joe saw the upper half of his brother's body disappear into the darkness above.

Suddenly Joe heard Frank give a cry of pain.

Seconds later Frank reeled backward, landing on top of Joe, and the two of them fell onto the floor.

Joe felt his head hit the floor, hard. Then everything went black.

3 A Surprise Guest

From far away, Joe heard Frank's voice say, "Joe! Are you okay? Joe!"

Joe opened his eyes and blinked. His brother's face slowly came into focus. Frank was leaning over him, a concerned expression on his face.

Joe raised a hand and gingerly felt the back of his head. He winced slightly when he found the lump that was starting to form. Then he got to his feet.

"You sure you're okay?" Frank asked anxiously.

"I'm fine," Joe replied. "But what about you?" he added, looking at the bruise on the side of Frank's head. There was also a small cut.

"It's okay," Frank said. "Just a little raw. Our friend in the attic was wearing good, solid boots, that's for sure. That's what he hit me with—his boot."

Joe gave a sigh. "I can't believe this. Our first day on the job and we're practically ready for the disabled list!"

"So what else is new?" Frank said with a grimace.

There was a knock at the door, and Steve Johnson stepped into the cabin.

"How're you guys—?" He stopped when he saw Frank's bruise.

Frank quickly explained what had happened.

"I want to take a look at that bruise," Steve said after Frank had finished. He reached into the top drawer of the bureau and pulled out a first-aid kit. "I put these kits in every cabin and room," he said. "Guests are always getting cuts and scrapes."

Frank sat on the edge of the bed.

"Did you manage to get a glimpse of the guy who attacked you?" Steve Johnson asked as he examined Frank's bruise.

Frank shook his head. "I didn't get a good look at him. It was dark up there, and he came at me from the side. I was pretty stunned after he hit me, and I fell. Then there was Joe to worry about."

Steve nodded. "I'd better check out that lump on the back of your head, Joe," he said.

"Sure, fine," Joe replied. "But first, I'm going to check out that attic." He grabbed a flashlight from his backpack. Then he dragged a wooden chair

24

over to the closet, stood on it, and pulled himself up into the attic.

Frank hissed a little as Steve applied iodine to the cut.

"Come on, don't be a sorehead," Joe joked as he swung down from the attic.

"Why don't you check around outside—far away outside," Frank growled.

When Joe returned, he let Steve look at the bump on his head.

"No real damage as far as I can tell," the lodge owner announced. "You'll both probably have headaches, but nothing a few aspirin won't cure. A little ice on these injuries might be a good idea."

Frank got up and opened the window. "Did you find anything?" he asked his brother as he plucked some of the bigger icicles hanging from the outside frame. He wrapped them in two towels Steve handed him.

Joe hesitated a moment before answering. "It's not much more than a crawl space up there," he said finally. "All I saw were trusses and insulation and electrical wires." He shot a sideways glance at his brother. Frank knew what that meant. Joe had seen more than he wanted to reveal right now.

"What do you usually keep up there, Steve?" asked Frank.

"Nothing, as far as I know," Steve replied.

"Anyway," continued Joe, "I know how the guy got away."

"He didn't come through here?" Frank asked.

Joe shook his head. "He kicked out the ventilation screen and jumped," he said. "I could see the grass matted right below it and some snapped branches on the bushes nearby." He shrugged. "The ground is covered with pine needles, and the underbrush gets really thick right away. There were no footprints and no way to track him down."

"Even if he didn't have a lead on us," Frank added grimly.

"The question is, who's our intruder?" said Joe.

"Well, the guests are all scattered throughout the woods," Steve said. "Any one of them could have come back."

"How about the staff?" Joe asked.

"Besides Willy, there's just my wife, Maggie, and my niece, Sara. I hope you don't seriously suspect my wife. Sara arrived from Boston yesterday. The two of them have been in the kitchen most of the day or with me. As for Willy"—Steve shrugged—"well, he was with me in the maintenance shack at the time of the attack." The lodge owner stood up. "Tell you what, it's getting close to dinnertime. Why don't you come up to the lodge and meet everyone—if you feel up to it."

"Why don't you give us a few more minutes with

26

this ice?" Frank suggested. "Joe, can you get me another towel?"

"Sure," said his brother. "We'll come up in a few minutes, okay, Steve?"

"Fine by me—take your time."

Steve closed the door gently.

"Are you really hurting?" Joe asked his brother. "Or did you catch my signal earlier, before I told Steve what I saw in the attic?"

"I caught it," Frank said. "And I wanted to ask you what you *really* saw when you looked around. I got the message that you were keeping something from Steve."

"I didn't want to give him more to worry about right now," Joe admitted. "But someone was definitely looking for something up there. There were a couple of square spaces that were free of dust—box shapes. I also found a lot of freshly torn cardboard scattered around, so the boxes are empty now. There was no sign of what was in them."

"The money from the robbery?" Frank guessed.

Joe shrugged. "Remember those fortune hunters Steve told us about? Wouldn't they have looked in the attic?"

"Maybe someone got a new clue. Anyhow, now we know we aren't dealing with a ghost. The guy who attacked me was human—with very big feet!" Frank got up and tossed the wet towel in the wash basin. "What do you say we meet the family circle?" He slid into his down jacket and headed for the door.

Joe grabbed his jacket and followed his brother into the cold night air.

When they reached the lodge porch, Steve and Willy were standing there, waiting for them.

"We're talking about the brake situation with the pickup truck," Steve told the Hardys as they stepped onto the porch.

Willy shook his head in puzzlement. "In all my days with the paper company, I never saw anything like it. And the mechanics who worked for the company were real experts. They had to be to work out here, miles away from a garage."

"Were you a logger?" Joe asked.

"No way!" Willy laughed. "I hated those chainsaws too much. I worked in maintenance for about fifteen years. Did some plumbing and electrical work at first, then I was mostly in the garage, keeping the heavy equipment working."

"Willy was getting ready to retire when I took over the lodge," Steve explained. "He's been here from day one."

"Can't figure any of this batch being able to mess around like mechanics," Willy said, still thinking about the brakes. "Especially that old man Peters and his nurse-companion, Fletcher. What do you think, Steve?"

28

Steve nodded in agreement. "I've never seen so many city slickers in one bunch of guests," he said. "These folks look like they have a hard time figuring which end of the gun the bullet comes out of. I'd hardly take them for mechanical types."

"Is the hunting bad?" Joe asked.

"Nah—but the hunters are," Willy said. "I bet some of them are up here just to take pictures."

"Come on," said Steve. "Let's go talk to Maggie and Sara. They're in the kitchen getting dinner ready. By the way, Sara doesn't know you're up here investigating. I didn't want to worry her."

He steered Frank and Joe into the lodge. As they passed through the living room, Steve greeted two men who were sitting there.

"Hello, Mr. Peters," he said, addressing an elderly man with thick glasses. "I hope you had a nice day."

"What's that?" asked Mr. Peters in a gravelly voice.

The bald, heavyset man sitting next to him said loudly, "He hopes you had a nice day!"

"Very nice," grunted Mr. Peters.

"I'd like you to meet some friends of mine," Steve said to the men. He introduced the Hardys.

"Pleased to meet you," said the bald man, whose name was Fletcher. Mr. Peters just nodded to Frank and Joe.

29

"Dinner will be ready soon," Steve told the men. Then he led Frank and Joe away toward the kitchen.

"They sure don't look like hunters to me," Joe said.

"They're not," replied Steve. "They're bird-watchers."

He pushed open a pair of swinging doors. Frank and Joe stepped into a large, well-organized kitchen. Spicy, inviting aromas filled the room.

A tall, attractive gray-haired woman was standing in front of the stove stirring a large pot of stew. She looked up and smiled at Steve and the Hardys. "You must be Frank and Joe," she said pleasantly. "I'm Maggie Johnson. Steve told me you were coming." Her smile faded a little. "I hope you'll be able to help us with our problem."

"We'll do our best, Maggie," Frank said seriously.

Just then, a door on one side of the room swung open, and a slim, pretty, blond teenage girl with her hair pulled back in a ponytail walked into the room, her arms filled with cans.

"Here, let me give you a hand," Joe said, stepping forward.

"Don't worry about Sara," Steve said. "She's a lot stronger than she looks."

"Thanks a lot, Uncle Steve," Sara said with a smile. She put the cans down on the counter in the middle of the room. "I have to be strong to get my work done around here."

"We're not working you too hard, are we, Sara?" Maggie asked.

"Well . . . not *that* hard," Sara said, her blue eyes twinkling.

"This young woman is Sara Benson, my niece, who will someday be a world-famous ballerina," Steve said to Frank and Joe. "Sara's on her fall break. She's up here helping Maggie with the laundry, the cleaning, making beds, and cooking."

"See why I'm so strong?" Sara said, giving her uncle a broad wink. "But I don't mind helping out at all. It's a nice change from school and ballet lessons. And it's so beautiful up here."

"I'm Frank Hardy and this is my brother, Joe," said Frank. "We're up here to do a story on the lodge and the Maine woods for our school paper."

"So we'll be wandering around, looking things over, if you don't mind," Joe put in.

"That's okay with me," said Sara. She grinned. "Actually, it's nice to meet a couple of guests who aren't interested in hunting."

"Yoo-hoo!" a voice called suddenly.

The Hardys, the Johnsons, and Sara looked toward the door.

A short, plump gray-haired man and woman stood in the half-open door, peering into the kitchen. They were both smiling brightly.

"We just thought we'd get some crackers and cheese to tide us over till dinner," the woman said.

"Oh, sure, Mrs. Ackerly," said Maggie. "Coming right up." She disappeared into the storeroom and came out with a hunk of golden yellow cheddar cheese and a large box of crackers.

"Mmm, that looks just *marvelous*," Mrs. Ackerly said in a gushing tone. "Doesn't it, Arthur?" She giggled. "But I'd better not eat too much of it. I've got to watch my waistline, you know. You're too good a cook, Maggie! Don't you think so, Arthur?"

Mr. Ackerly opened his mouth to reply, but before he could say anything, his wife said, "Now, just give the cheese to me, Maggie. I'll set it up in the living room. You've got enough to do. Come on, Arthur." She took the cheese, crackers, and a knife and left the kitchen, her husband following closely behind.

"And those are the Ackerlys," Steve said.

"Whew," said Joe. "Does Mr. Ackerly ever manage to get a word in edgewise?"

Steve chuckled. "Sometimes." He looked at his watch. "Listen, I'm going to stop in my office to see if some new reservations I'm expecting came through on the answering machine. I'll be back in a few minutes." He left the kitchen.

"We'd better get the show on the road," Maggie said briskly. "I'm not convinced that hunk of cheese is going to tide anyone over. Especially not

Adele Ackerly!" She and Sara grabbed a stack of plates, napkins, and silverware.

"Here, let us help you with that," said Frank.

"Grab those salt and pepper shakers," said Maggie. "And those bread baskets."

"And the ketchup bottles and the hot sauce," added Sara as she bustled out of the kitchen.

With the four of them setting up the dining room, it didn't take long before it was ready for the hungry guests.

"Now all we need is some milk to fill these pitchers," Maggie announced as she led them back into the kitchen.

Joe helped Sara put the pitchers on a tray. Frank followed Maggie toward the storeroom, pausing to pop a warm biscuit into his mouth on the way. He heard the heavy handle to the walk-in refrigerator open. Then came a loud shriek.

Frank hurried over to the refrigerator just in time to catch Maggie as she reeled backward. She collapsed in his arms.

Joe rushed over to help, but Frank shook his head. "I've got her. See what's in there!"

Joe worked his way around them, peered inside the refrigerator, and gasped.

Hanging on one of the meathooks was the limp body of what appeared to be a headless man!

4 Deadly Games

Joe stared at the figure in the refrigerator. After a moment, he realized what he was really looking at. He smiled grimly and shook his head.

"Some joke," he muttered.

Meanwhile, Frank had moved Maggie back and was trying to ease her into a chair. Sara came through the kitchen door. "We need some— Hey, what's going on?"

She turned toward the open refrigerator door, but Frank called, "Grab a chair and help me get Maggie down."

Sara helped Frank get Maggie seated, then said, "I'd better get Steve."

A moment later, Steve was in the kitchen. He knelt next to his wife and patted her hand until she

34

came to. "The freezer!" Maggie said with a start, her eyes going wide with fright. "Someone—"

"It's okay, Maggie," Frank said in a reassuring tone. He had looked in the refrigerator after Steve had arrived. "It's not a real person."

"It's a dummy," said Joe, leaning out of the walk-in refrigerator.

"A dummy?" Maggie sat up in the chair.

"Exactly." Joe stepped out of the refrigerator. He was holding a limp form in his arms. "See, it's just a bunch of old clothes stuffed with leaves and rags and— Well, well, look at this!"

He pulled out some fluffy padding and held it up.

"What's that yellow stuff?" Sara asked.

"Insulation," Joe replied. "Our mysterious friend is a local boy. Part of him came from our cabin's attic."

"You know, those clothes look kind of familiar, too," said Steve.

"Right." Maggie turned to the Hardys. "Are you in cabin seven?"

Frank and Joe nodded.

"I stored a box of old clothes from our lost and found up in the attic there," Maggie said, turning to Steve. "Remember? They were in your office for ages. In fact, I warned everyone at breakfast this morning not to forget anything or that's where it would end up."

"That explains a few things," said Joe. "Just somebody's idea of a practical joke. When do you think the dummy was put in the refrigerator?"

"It could have been anytime after breakfast," said Maggie. "I was working in another part of the lodge all morning and didn't come into the kitchen until lunchtime. Then I was in the office, going over the bills, until dinnertime. I didn't need anything from that refrigerator until now."

"I was making beds and cleaning in the morning. I spent the afternoon in the laundry room in back of the kitchen," said Sara. "I didn't notice anyone coming or going."

"Well, we'd better dump this, then come back for dinner," said Joe.

"Let's not play into this joker's hands," Frank suggested. "We won't give him the satisfaction of even mentioning that we found the dummy, okay?"

The Johnsons and Sara agreed. The two women continued their final preparations for dinner as the boys carried the dummy out back to the Dumpster near the maintenance shed.

"Good thing Maggie keeled over before she got a good look," said Joe the minute they were alone outside. "She didn't see this."

He held out a piece of brown paper.

"It was pinned on top, right where the head should have been," he continued. "Read it."

36

Frank looked at the crude printing: "Get those kids out of here or else."

"This was probably meant for Steve's eyes," said Frank. "Why didn't you show it to him?"

"For the same reason I didn't say anything about the torn-up box in the attic. He has enough to worry about. And Maggie and Sara are jittery enough as it is," Joe explained.

"I guess you're right. One thing's for sure," Frank said. "Someone doesn't want us around."

"But how did that someone find out who we are?" Joe wanted to know.

"He or she must have been listening in on our conversation with Steve in the dining room earlier," Frank said.

Joe glanced at the dummy. "Maybe we ought to take a closer look at our scarecrow friend to see if there's anything else he can tell us."

"We don't want to be too late for dinner. It'll look funny," said Frank. "Let's just stick him in that little tool shed next to the Dumpster. We can come back later and really go over him."

"Okay," Joe agreed. "Come on, Scarecrow, time for your nap."

They propped up the dummy against a wall inside the tool shed and shut the door. Then they went back into the lodge. As they stepped inside, they saw Steve come out of his office off the living room.

"Two reservations for next week cancelled," Steve said, walking up to them. "The cancellees heard that something funny was going on up here." He shook his head. "It just keeps getting worse. Maybe I ought to close down for the season."

"Hang in there, Steve," said Frank. "Some of these so-called accidents and practical jokes may give us clues. First thing tomorrow morning, we're going to comb the area and see if we can tie anything we find to what's been going on."

"Give us a chance," Joe said. "I mean, we just got here."

"I know," Steve said with a sigh. "But I don't know how much more of this I can take."

"Don't get discouraged," Joe said. He smiled. "Remember, a happy innkeeper . . ."

"Keeps his head?" Steve finished, with a slight grin, as they stepped into the dining room.

Most of the guests were already seated around the long trestle table. Steve had started to introduce Frank and Joe when three more guests came in.

Steve introduced the Hardys to the late arrivals. They were middle-aged businessmen from Providence, whose names were Mr. Brown, Mr. Burns, and Mr. Buckley.

"We call them the Three B's," Steve told Frank and Joe.

Brown was stocky, Buckley was tall and thin, and Burns was short, with an angry squint.

38

Frank and Joe noticed that the trio looked as if they rarely spent any time outdoors. Buckley and Brown were very pale, while Burns had the red face that usually went with someone who was always angry—or had high blood pressure.

The businessmen had little to say beyond grunts of acknowledgment as they started to take their seats.

Suddenly Burns jumped back. "Forget it! I can't sit at this table," he announced.

"What's the matter, Burnsie?" asked Mr. Buckley as he eased his tall, lean frame into his chair.

"Thirteen," Burns replied. "There'll be thirteen at the table. That's unlucky. I can't eat here."

"Oh, come now, Mr. Burns," Mrs. Ackerly said. "You don't believe in such nonsense, do you? We certainly don't, do we, Arthur?"

"Right," a weedy-looking young man named Len Randall put in. "You can't let a silly superstition ruin your meal."

But Burns just shook his head firmly, his squint deepening. "Bad luck is bad luck. That's not what I need."

"Calm down, Burnsie," said Buckley in a low voice. "There's still another empty chair."

Maggie walked in from the kitchen with a pitcher of cold water. She sat down at the end of the table. Burns's red face turned even redder with embar-

39

rassment. "I've had enough of the number thirteen," he muttered as he sat down.

Now, what was *that* all about? Frank wondered to himself. Why was Burns so upset by the number thirteen?

The guests began to chat with each other in a friendly manner.

Mrs. Ackerly mentioned that she and her husband were hunting live game for the first time. "But I've got quite a reputation as a champion skeet and trap shooter, if I do say so myself." She buttered a roll and popped it into her mouth.

"Clay pigeons are much more predictable," said Mr. Ackerly, who was finally getting a word in edgewise, now that his wife was busy eating. "But my wife wants to try her hand at bigger game. Maybe we'll spot a moose."

"It's possible but not probable," said Len Randall. He was a young reporter for *All Outdoors*, the popular nature magazine. "The moose is making a comeback, but it's pretty slow."

"We sure would love to get a good picture of a moose for our feature on the Maine woods," said Randall's colleague, Mike Mallory, a staff photographer who looked even younger than Randall. Both men were out on their first big story assignment.

"So far all we've got is a bunch of migrating birds," said Randall.

"That ought to make things interesting for you, Mr. Peters," said Steve.

The elderly gentleman looked up from the far end of the table, where he sat hunched over his plate. He peered over at Steve through his thick glasses. Then he turned to Mr. Fletcher, who was seated next to him, and asked, "What's that he said, Fletcher?"

In a loud voice, Fletcher said, "Birds. He says they've got a lot of interesting migrating birds out there."

"Oh, yes, right," Mr. Peters said, nodding. "We came to see the birds as they head south."

He bent his head and returned to his meal as the others discussed their various plans for bagging a trophy.

When dinner was over, the Three B's went upstairs to their rooms. Randall and Mallory left for their cabin. Mr. Peters asked Fletcher to accompany him to the lakeside. Before retiring to their cabin, he wanted to see if he could spot any night birds by moonlight.

Mr. and Mrs. Ackerly took their coffee mugs and settled down beside the roaring fire in the living room.

Frank and Joe headed for the living room, too.

"Not much evening entertainment for young people, I'm afraid," Mrs. Ackerly said, smiling at Frank

41

and Joe. "There might just be a show tomorrow morning, though," she added with a nervous giggle.

Frank and Joe glanced at each other. Mrs. Ackerly was obviously expecting to see the ghost drive by in the morning.

"We could try our hand at darts," her husband suggested, quickly changing the subject.

"Why not?" Frank said. "We'll take you on."

"All right," Mrs. Ackerly said. Then she added with a simper, "Although I'm *sure* I'm no match for you young men."

It didn't take long to discover that Mrs. Ackerly was more than a match for the Hardy brothers. Mr. Ackerly was a so-so dart thrower. His wife, however, could have been a professional.

"Rematch?" Joe asked, despite the heavy odds against winning.

"Right after I come back from the kitchen," Mrs. Ackerly said. "I need more coffee and some of Maggie's delectable chocolate-chip cookies." She stepped behind the overstuffed sofa that faced the dart board and left the room.

Frank flopped down on the sofa and gave a sigh. "You'd think her darts had magnetic tips the way they found the bull's-eye," he said.

"Radar," suggested Joe, seated at the other end of the sofa. "She uses radar."

42

"Or maybe it's witchcraft," Frank said with a grin.

"Adele is just an ordinary mortal, like you and me," Mr. Ackerly said with a laugh, as he sat down between them.

He looked down at the score pad on the coffee table in front of him.

"If you boys are going to make a comeback, maybe you ought to practice," he suggested.

"Good idea," Frank said. He picked up the pile of darts from the table. With his back to the sofa and the doorway leading from the dining room, he started throwing darts at the target.

"Well, at least they're all inside the big circle," said Joe. "I guess I'll just have to show you how it's done."

Joe strolled up to the board. "Keep score for me," he said as he reached up to retrieve the darts Frank had thrown.

The clattering sound of the pencil dropping on the coffee table made Joe turn his head.

Then he caught the gleam of shiny metal as it whizzed through the air and headed straight for his heart!

5 Night Stalking

Joe felt his feet fly out from under him.

He fell sideways. As he dropped, a loud *thunk!* rang out. Then Joe hit the bare floor in front of the dart board—hard.

"Ouch!" he shouted, rubbing his bruised hip. "What happened?"

Mr. Ackerly stood over him, his face gray. "Your —your brother pulled the rug out from under you," he said. "He probably saved your life!" He pointed at the dart board.

Joe looked up and stared at the dart board.

Right in the middle of the bull's-eye, buried halfway to the hilt, was a hunting knife. In the soft light of the lounge, it seemed to shimmer—as though it were still vibrating from the impact.

44

Frank kicked aside the crumpled throw rug next to Joe and hurried over to his brother.

"Are you all right?" he asked anxiously.

"I'm fine," Joe said. He got to his feet. "Thanks to your fast thinking. That was a close one!"

"I wouldn't want to try that rug-pulling stunt a second time," Frank admitted.

"You have good reflexes, Frank," said Mr. Ackerly, a little color coming back to his cheeks. "I barely dropped the pencil, and you made your move."

"So that was you I heard—" Joe started to say.

"Having fun, boys?" Mrs. Ackerly asked brightly, as she strolled into the room. She was carrying a mug of coffee and a cloth napkin.

She stopped when she found her husband and the two boys staring at her.

"What's the matter? You three look as though you've seen a ghost," she said with a laugh.

"You couldn't—I mean, I can't imagine—" her husband stammered.

"Stop stammering, Arthur," she ordered briskly. "What's going on?"

"Someone just happened to throw a knife at Joe while he was standing at the dart board," Frank told her. "It had to come from the direction of the dining room."

"You can't believe that I—" she began. Her

round face turned red. "But no one else was in the dining room. I've never been so insulted in my life!"

"Take it easy, dear," said her husband. "No one is accusing you. Anyone could have been in the dining room or the hallway. All of us had our backs to that doorway."

Frank and Joe had to admit that Mr. Ackerly was right. They had all been so absorbed in what was going on at the dart board, anyone might have quietly slipped in behind them and thrown the knife. In the confusion afterward, the knife thrower could easily have fled through the kitchen or slipped out of the lodge through the hallway.

"Really, I can't imagine why you would accuse me—*me*," Mrs. Ackerly continued. "Why, I—"

"I think we'd better go to our cabin, Adele," interrupted Mr. Ackerly. "I don't think we should stay here. Who knows what could happen next. Maybe you boys ought to leave, too."

"You go ahead," Frank said. "We'll just take a quick look around."

Mr. Ackerly put an arm around his wife's shoulders and led her away.

Frank went over to the target and looked at the knife.

"Nothing special," he told Joe. "Standard hunting knife. Everyone in the place probably has one. I'll bet Steve even keeps a few extras around."

46

"Fingerprints?" Joe asked.

"Looks pretty clean," Frank said. "If Mrs. Ackerly is the knife thrower, she could have held the knife with her cloth napkin. The napkin would have kept prints off the knife." He gave a shrug. "But even if we found some prints on the knife, how would we check them against everybody here?"

"You're right about that. But let's hold on to it anyway. You never know. And it'll be evidence, if we—"

"If? Let's talk about *when*," Frank interrupted.

"Okay, okay, *when* we solve this case," said Joe. He paused for a moment, then asked, "Do you think whoever did it is still hanging around?"

"No, but let's check out the area. Maybe we'll find something. Why don't you take the dining room area. I'll see if I can find anything near the front door," Frank suggested.

For the next fifteen minutes, the brothers carefully checked the dining room and hallway.

They met back in the living room.

"I found cookie crumbs on the dining room floor, but that's about it," Joe declared. "But I'm positive that Mrs. Ackerly was in the dining room recently. I smelled her perfume right outside the door."

"So she could have thrown the knife from the hall, then slipped into the dining room and kitchen," said Frank. "And maybe Arthur dropped the

47

pencil as some sort of signal. Which means the two of them were in it together."

Joe shook his head. "I don't know, Frank. That knife was thrown pretty hard. I mean, it was halfway into the board! Mrs. Ackerly probably has the aim, but I'm not convinced she could have put that much muscle behind it." He turned to his brother. "So, did you find anything in there?"

"Just what you'd suspect," Frank answered. "Lots of wet marks on the doormat and on the coat rack. Anyone could have been out there during the last hour or so."

"Well, at least we know it wasn't our headless pal out back," said Joe. "Which reminds me, we'd better get rid of him before he turns up somewhere else or before someone finds him."

"After that, I think we should start checking out the rest of our fellow guests," said Frank. "Quietly. And discreetly, of course."

They left the lodge and headed for the tool shed next to the Dumpster. The dummy was propped up against the wall, exactly the way the Hardys had left him.

As they carried the dummy out, Joe nodded over toward the maintenance shack. There were no lights in the windows on the second level.

"Willy turns in right after dinner," he said. "Steve was talking about that at dinner. He says you can set your watch by the time Willy goes to bed and gets up. There's no real reason to believe that he was prowling around the lodge. Someone might have noticed him."

"He's not off my suspect list yet," Frank said. "His reaction to the brake failure was a little funny, if you ask me. He seemed more astonished by it than worried."

The boys knelt down and examined the dummy carefully, taking out its stuffing bit by bit.

"Looks like your basic dummy to me," said Frank, holding a handful up for inspection. "Old clothes, stuffing . . ."

"The only thing I can see is that whoever put him together did it fast," Joe commented. "The stuffing is just leaves, rags, and that insulation."

Frank nodded. "This looks like it was a rush job to me, too. The dummy maker probably wanted to get the message to us as quickly as possible." Frank pushed the stuffing back into the dummy and straightened up. "Well, the message was received, but we're not taking its advice. We're not leaving!"

"So I guess it's time to give Scarecrow the old heave-ho," said Joe.

Smiling to each other, the brothers each grabbed an arm and a leg. As they hefted the dummy high over the lid and into the dumpster, Frank said loudly, "That ought to settle the score, Lefty."

49

"Yeah, tell all your friends," Joe said with a laugh.

"Now let's see if we can check a few names off our list," Frank said as they turned back toward the lodge.

"The Three B's are the only guests staying in the main lodge, right?" Joe asked in a low voice as they entered the building.

"Plus Steve and Maggie and Sara," Frank replied. "But I doubt Steve's own family is out to make trouble for him. It doesn't make sense."

They checked the mailboxes in the hallway to see which guest was in which room.

Then they crept up the staircase that stood at the far end of the living room, opposite the dining room. Noiselessly, they walked down the hallway.

The brothers stopped outside the only room occupied by the Three B's that had any sound or light coming through the cracks. Joe knelt down and screwed his eye up next to the keyhole.

The room was thick with cigar smoke and Joe could see the Three B's sitting at a table. They were muttering in low voices.

He straightened up and led Frank away from the door.

"Would you believe it?" Joe whispered. "They're playing cards. Poker, I think."

"Poker?"

"Well, there're chips and cards all over the table.

50

I can't tell how long the game has been going on," said Joe.

"So much for the Three B's," said Frank.

"Let's go check out the cabins," Joe suggested.

They crept back down the stairs and out of the main lodge.

The first cabin they passed housed Peters and Fletcher. Through the windows they could see Mr. Peters listening to a miniature personal stereo. The bird watcher leaned forward in his chair, frowning in concentration.

"Probably checking out bird calls," Joe whispered below the windowsill.

"The bald hulk—what's his name?" Frank began.

"Fletcher," said Joe.

"Looks like he's got the remote control box for a model airplane in there," Frank continued. "Maybe he's planning to knock off a few feathered friends the hard way."

"Well, it's pretty obvious he's not a bird lover like Peters," said Joe. "But maybe he's just a kid at heart who likes playing with gadgets like that."

They moved on to the cabin shared by Mallory and Randall.

All sorts of photographic equipment was spread out on both beds. Mallory was assembling something that looked a little like a drill press.

"That's an enlarger," whispered Frank. "He

probably has the makings of a complete darkroom there." He looked around the room. "But where's Randall? I don't see him."

"I'll try the bathroom window," said Joe, moving around the corner. He returned immediately. "No, he's not there."

"Now that's very interesting," said Frank. "Maybe he's back at the lodge. In fact . . ."

"Maybe, just maybe, he's been there the whole evening," Joe finished.

"Let's go back to the lodge," said Frank. "If Randall's there, I want to find out if he was the one who decided to use you for target practice."

The Hardy brothers made their way back to the lodge. As they entered, they could see a line of light coming from under the door to Steve's office.

"That light wasn't on before," Joe whispered.

Trying to move without making a sound, the Hardys inched toward the door and eased it open a crack. They were just in time to hear someone speak into the telephone.

"I want to report a murder!"

6 Ghostly Doings

The door creaked as Joe pushed it open. The telephone clattered to the floor as the caller gasped and whirled around to face the Hardys.

It was Len Randall.

At the sight of Frank and Joe standing in the doorway, he backed away in terror.

"Don't come near me!" he screamed. "Murderers!"

"What are you talking about?" Joe asked. "Are you nuts?"

"I saw what you did! But you won't g-g-get away with it!" Randall stammered. "I—I know where the body is!"

"The body?" Frank said in a puzzled tone. Then his eyes lit up. "Oh, you mean the *dummy*." He turned to Joe. "He saw us dumping the dummy!"

Joe burst out laughing, but Randall didn't see anything funny about it. His eyes darted back and forth between the Hardys, while his hands clenched into fists. "Don't try anything funny," he said nervously. "The police are on their way."

Joe picked up the phone, dialed 911, and apologized to the operator for Randall's call.

Meanwhile, Frank tried to explain to Randall that what he had seen was a dummy. "Just a harmless practical joke," he finished. "Maggie made it to give Steve a laugh," Frank added untruthfully.

"We didn't want to spread it around because it was a joke just between them. Because it's going to be part of our story, I guess we can let you in on it," said Joe.

"Right," Frank said, picking up the cue. "We're not up here hunting, we're doing a story for our school paper about a trip to the Maine woods. A kind of writing assignment."

Randall still looked as if he weren't ready to believe them. It took a while for the Hardys to convince him that they were unarmed and harmless. Finally, they led him out back to the Dumpster. Forming a four-arm hoist, they lifted the reporter up so he could peek in and see the dummy with its stuffing spilled out all over the Dumpster.

"I guess you guys are on the level," Randall

admitted, after the Hardys had eased him back onto the ground.

He began to talk more freely as they walked toward the cabins.

"Too bad it wasn't a real murder," he said with a sigh. "I could have used the story."

"For a nature magazine?" Frank asked.

"I might as well let you in on a little secret, too," Randall said finally. "That *All Outdoors* thing is just a cover. Mike Mallory and I really work for *In the Know.*"

"The scandal sheet?" Joe explained. "That's the newspaper that prints those really stupid headlines like 'Invisible Aliens from Mars Are Walking Among Us.'"

"Hey, you've got to start somewhere," Randall said, looking offended. "This is my first job as a reporter. I used to sell classified ads. But I managed to sell one of the editors on the idea of doing a story on this place."

He lowered his voice as he went on. "A bunch of bank robbers holed up here once—three got caught, and one disappeared. The editor liked it, so Mike and I got a shot at a filler story. You know— 'Ten Years Later: The Ghost of Lakeside Lodge!' That kind of thing helps sell papers."

"But there isn't any ghost," Joe quickly pointed out.

"Oh, it's all in the way you write it," Randall

said. "I mean, you have to exaggerate a *little*. Anyway, I think I've got enough material to start writing a good story."

Frank and Joe looked at each other unhappily. This kind of publicity was just what Steve *didn't* need.

"They sent you all the way out here just for that?" asked Frank. "With a photographer? Mallory is a photographer, isn't he?"

"Oh, sure. And he's almost as interested in that old robbery as I am," Randall said. "But I have him beat. I have a whole folder on the crime. Newspaper clippings, the works."

"You know, I'd really like to see that file sometime," Frank said casually. "It would be great to pick up a few pointers from a real pro."

Joe bit his lip to hide a smile.

"Forget it. I'm not about to give away all my secrets," Randall said jealously, scurrying down the path. "You might try to sell my story to one of our competitors!" He slammed his cabin door behind him.

"Like what?" Joe said, scowling. *"The Weekly Fishwrap News?"*

Frank just shook his head as they followed the path to cabin seven.

"I wish we could see that file," he muttered as they entered their own cabin.

* * *

56

When the Hardys arrived at the breakfast table the next morning, all the other guests were already eating—except the Ackerlys and Steve.

Joe went into the kitchen for some fresh coffee. "Where's Steve?" he asked Maggie.

She poured him a cup and shook her head.

"Mr. Ackerly came in bright and early and told Steve that he and his wife wanted to check out. He asked Steve to get Jerry Barnes to come for them. Steve wanted to know why, but Mr. A. wouldn't say. So Steve got some coffee and toast together and went off to cabin five—that's where the Ackerlys are staying. He's probably still there," she said.

Joe returned to the dining room and found the guests preparing to set off for a day's hunting and hiking. He and Frank finished their scrambled eggs and sausage. They carried their plates and mugs into the kitchen, then headed outside.

"I didn't notice you boys saying what you were planning to do today," said Willy, who was sweeping off the front porch.

"Oh, we're going to take it kind of easy," Frank told the caretaker. "I don't want to try any heavy-duty hiking until I know the area better."

"Yeah, since this is our first day, we'll keep pretty close to the lake shore," added Joe.

"Still, you'd better have a map," Willy said. He

reached into his jacket pocket and pulled out a printed copy of the Lakeside Lodge property. Then he left the porch and headed for the maintenance shed.

Frank and Joe noticed that the guests hesitated a bit as they started off into the woods. They all glanced sideways and over their shoulders, as if they were expecting something to happen.

"The ghost apparently didn't show up this morning," said Joe. "Or if it did, nobody's talking about it."

"They haven't talked much about the ghost at all," Frank said. "But it seems like they all believe in it."

Steve came up to them, shaking his head. "I just had a long session with the Ackerlys. Mrs. A. was all for going off hunting. Her husband was very upset, but he wouldn't say why." The lodge owner sighed. "At least I talked them into sticking around awhile longer."

Frank and Joe told him about the knife-throwing incident.

"No wonder Mr. A. wanted out of here," Steve said, shaking his head. "Well, it's a good thing Mrs. Ackerly is the good-natured type. And fortunately she's hot to nail a prize trophy deer. I convinced her that people get lucky toward the end of the week, so they're going to stay. But I don't know how much longer I can hold out without getting in touch with the state police."

"I guess we should also tell you about Randall and Mallory," said Frank.

When Frank had finished, Steve looked very unhappy. "Publicity like that will just about do us in. We'll have to close down."

"Don't do anything drastic yet, Steve," said Frank. "We're going to turn on the steam. First, we'll let everyone see us heading off along the shore, just the way we said we would. Then we'll double back here and go over this place inch by inch."

"We're bound to turn up something," Joe added reassuringly.

Steve's face brightened a bit and he managed a smile. "Okay, I won't give up yet," he said. "Let me know if I can do anything to help." Then he headed into the lodge.

"Hey, where's your red vest?" Frank asked Joe as they set off for the lake shore. "You know it's dangerous to be out in hunting country without one."

Joe announced, "I've got something better."

He reached into his pocket and pulled out a very long, bright red wool scarf.

"Iola knitted it for me—for my birthday," Joe said. Iola was Chet Morton's sister. She and Joe had been dating steadily for a long time. "I haven't had a chance to use it until now, but it should do the job."

"Right—as long as it holds together," Frank said, looking at the loosely woven wool. "Anyway, we could always use it as a marker line, from here to where we're going, in case we get lost. It's long enough!"

"Skip the wisecracks, okay?" said Joe. "Let's get down to business. First of all, do you think we should both double back and search the lodge? Maybe I should tail some of the guests to see what they're up to."

By now they were well out of sight of the lodge. Soon they were walking on a dirt road that ran by the lake. An eerie mist rose from the water. Waves gently lapped at the shore.

"Don't you want to see if our ghost shows up?" Frank asked.

"Come on, Frank," said Joe. "You don't believe in ghosts any more than I do, and—"

"Do you believe in chainsaws?" Frank asked suddenly. "It sounds as if someone's cutting some wood right nearby."

"It's getting closer," said Joe. "Hey, you don't move that fast using a chainsaw." He whirled around, staring back down the dirt road. "It's coming from behind us!"

60

The drone of an engine grew louder and louder.

Joe's eyes widened and Frank's jaw dropped as they saw a tall, shrouded figure in white appear out of the early morning mist.

The figure in white gave a bloodcurdling yell as it moved toward them at top speed!

7 The Heat Is On

The figure revved up the engine on the ATV.

Instinctively, Joe raised an arm to signal the driver to stop. Frank just grabbed his brother, jerking him off the road as the "ghost" rushed by.

The rapid movement sent the Hardys reeling backward—into the shallow water at the edge of the lake.

Joe scrambled to his feet, dripping and sputtering. "That water's cold!" he exclaimed as he sloshed out of the lake.

"Now I know why they call this season fall," Frank said with a shiver. "That seems to be all we're doing here. Falling!"

The brothers were in no condition to pursue the driver of the ATV. Instead, chilled and shivering, they hurried back to their cabin to dry off and change their clothes.

Their next stop was Steve's office, where they told the lodge owner about their mysterious close encounter.

"That's strange," Steve said. "It's a little late in the day for our friend's appearance. And he usually drives past the lodge."

Suddenly they heard a loud voice say, "Aha! I've got you now, Arthur!" The Hardys and Steve looked into the living room and saw the Ackerlys seated at a small table near the roaring fire.

Mrs. Ackerly slapped down a card and exclaimed, "Gin!"

"Oh, no, not again," Mr. Ackerly said with a groan. He frowned and started counting the cards in his hand.

"So much for big game hunting," Joe murmured.

"Anyway, this little adventure taught us one thing," said Frank. "Our ghost definitely knows how to handle an ATV. I never knew those things could go so fast!"

Joe nodded. "That guy in white was either a stunt driver or someone wild enough to risk a big splash."

"But the big question is still *who* did it?" said Steve. "We can ask Maggie and Sara if they've seen anyone prowling around in a white sheet, but I doubt if they have. They'd have said something.

63

Both of them have been in and out of here, cleaning up and going over supplies with me since breakfast."

"What about Willy?" asked Joe.

"He's been up to his elbows in grease getting our bulldozer in shape," Steve said. "That old logging road leading away from the cabins is a mess. A whole bunch of trees fell down during the last big storm we had. Willy's going to try to clean it up."

"And the Ackerlys?" asked Frank. "Were they here all morning?"

"As far as I can tell," Steve said. "She's been walloping him at gin rummy from the sound of it."

"That pretty much narrows it down to the group out in the woods. Peters and Fletcher, Randall and Mallory, and the Three B's." Frank shook his head. "That's still a lot of people to account for."

"Too many for just the two of us to keep an eye on," Joe said. "You know what I'm thinking?"

Frank nodded. "Chet and Biff," he said. "They're not doing anything else as far as I know — not since we wrecked their vacation."

"Who?" asked Steve.

"Some really good friends of ours who have helped us out with cases in the past," Joe explained. "It's obvious that someone knows who we are and why we're here. That makes it tougher for us to do our job."

"Right," Frank said. "Chet and Biff don't have to pass themselves off as hunters—not all of your guests are here to hunt. They could pretend to be heavy-duty hiker types."

"'Pretend' is the right word," Frank muttered under his breath.

"They could follow the guests and maybe pick up some clues," Joe continued, ignoring Frank's comment. "I'd say it's worth giving them a call."

"Sounds good to me," Steve said. "The more help we have with this problem, the better."

Just then, Sara walked into Steve's office. She was holding a small pair of binoculars.

"Did either of you guys leave these in the dining room?" she asked Frank and Joe. "I found them while I was cleaning off the sideboard."

The Hardys shook their heads.

"I'll put them on the table by the front door," said Steve. "That's where people pick up messages or mail."

"While you're doing that, I'll take care of that telephone call," said Frank.

"Help yourself," Steve said, nodding toward the phone. "Come on, Sara, let's get out of the man's way."

Frank picked up the receiver and dialed Chet's number in Bayport. The phone rang several times before Chet finally answered. Frank filled Chet in on the situation and gave him instructions on how to get to Lakeside Lodge. Then he called Biff and repeated the information.

"Well?" Joe asked impatiently. "What's the story?"

"Reinforcements are on the way. But not until tomorrow. That's the earliest they can get here," Frank told his brother. "They're both really excited about coming up here," he added with a smile. "But I warned them not to let on that they knew us. They're supposed to be a couple of young, eager hikers."

Joe laughed. "We'd better get out the blister ointment," he suggested. "To Chet and Biff, 'hike' is a word you say in a football game."

"Meanwhile, this is our chance to take a good look around the area. Let's start with the Ackerlys' cabin while they're busy playing cards," Frank suggested.

The Hardy brothers left the lodge and made their way down the path to cabin five. A quick but thorough search turned up nothing unusual. They headed for the cabin shared by Randall and Mallory.

"Locked," Joe said disgustedly as he rattled the doorknob. He knocked on the door several times, but there was no answer.

"The shades are drawn, too," Frank said. "The

question is, do these guys really have something to hide, or are they just protecting their story?"

Next, they searched the cabin occupied by Peters, the elderly bird watcher, and his companion, Fletcher.

"I guess Fletcher is really into model airplane flying," Frank commented, as he stared at the box which contained wires, diodes, soldering tools, a small pair of pliers, and plastic parts. A model airplane sat on the dresser. "He sure has a lot of electronics stuff here."

"Peters must really love birds," Joe commented. "Look at all the books he's got on the subject. I can't believe an old guy like that would want to tramp around the woods in this cold weather."

He picked up a sheet of transparent paper off the bed. It had alphabetical markings on it. "A, B, C, D, E, F, G, H . . ." read Joe.

"Some of the letters have been crossed off," said Frank, looking over his brother's shoulder.

"Probably something to do with bird calls, musical notes or something like that," Joe said with a shrug.

"That does it." Frank sighed. "We've been through just about every nook and cranny, even the empty attics in these cabins."

"Let's check the Three B's' rooms in the lodge," Joe said. "And we should hit Willy's room over the maintenance shack."

"What about that tool shed where we first stashed the dummy?" asked Frank. "We never really got a good look around there."

Joe nodded. "Why don't you poke around in there while I check out the rooms in the lodge? We don't have a lot of time—before you know it, they'll all be back, looking for lunch."

The Hardys left the cabin and headed for the lodge. Frank headed toward the area out back.

He glanced around to make sure no one was watching. Then he opened the door of the tool shed and stepped inside. He shut the door behind him. That will give me some privacy, Frank thought.

With the door closed, there wasn't much light in the windowless shack, just a few tiny rays of sunlight poking through the cracks.

Frank took out his pocket flashlight, switched it on, and shone it around the room.

There was a pile of old rags in the room that looked like the rags Frank and Joe had found inside the dummy. Rusting tin cans and wastepaper took up most of the floor space. Frank picked up one of the cans. Stuffed inside was a wadded-up piece of paper that was just beginning to turn yellow around the edges.

Frank smoothed out the paper and looked at it. He recognized it as another copy of the Lakeside Lodge map. This copy had a dark X placed in three different areas. Suddenly, the glint of shiny metal caught his eye. He bent over and pulled a small folding shovel from underneath some of the rusty cans.

Maybe I should take a better look under these cans, Frank thought. He knelt down and began to rummage through the pile.

Suddenly, he began to feel warmer. At first he thought it was from the closeness of the small space, but then a familiar smell drifted into the shed. Frank sniffed the air.

Smoke.

There must be a fire nearby, Frank thought. I'd better take a look.

He pushed against the door, but it wouldn't budge.

Frank scowled. Just what he needed—a stuck door. He shoved again, and it wobbled just a tiny bit.

The heat was growing more intense. By now the smell of smoke had gotten very strong.

Frank hurled himself against the door now, but it remained shut. With a sinking feeling, he realized that the door must have been locked from the outside.

Along the floorboards under his feet, tiny flames were starting to leap up into the shed.

The cabin was on fire!

8 Up for Air

"Help!" Frank yelled. He pounded on the thick wooden walls of the shed, but they wouldn't give.

The smoke grew thicker and the heat more intense. Frank frantically searched the small building for any sign of an opening, but the boards had all been nailed tight. There was no way out except for the barred door.

Frank began banging on the walls with the small shovel he'd found. It didn't even make a dent in the wood. Frank continued to hit the walls and he started yelling again. He hoped someone would hear him.

The smoke was getting denser. Frank's blows against the wall became weaker and weaker. His shouts for help ended in a spasm of coughing and his eyes stung.

Frank dropped the shovel and staggered back against one wall, stumbling over the cans and debris. It was getting harder and harder to breathe, and he was very dizzy. He slid down the wall onto the floor and felt himself start to slip into unconsciousness.

Suddenly, Frank felt an icy blast of cold air on his face. The shock cleared his head just in time. He rolled sideways as part of the wall in front of him came crashing down.

Frank blinked in surprise. The gigantic metal blade of an old-fashioned bulldozer was staring him in the face.

"What, in the name of Mike, are *you* doing in there?" bellowed a familiar voice from behind the metal blade.

"Willy!" Frank yelled above the roar of an engine. "Back that thing up!"

The bulldozer slowly pulled away. Frank quickly scrambled out of the hole in the smoke-filled shed.

He saw Joe hurrying toward them from the lodge.

Willy turned off the engine and climbed out of the cab of the big bulldozer.

Frank gulped in lungfuls of clean air and began to feel much better.

"Hey, kid, are you all right?"

"Frank! Are you okay?" Joe asked as he rushed up to his brother.

When Frank nodded that he was fine, the mainte-

71

nance man's expression changed from worry to anger. "Going in there was a pretty dumb thing to do, kid," Willy said shortly.

"Oh, yeah?" Frank snapped. "How about you not taking a look inside the shed before you locked it?"

"For all we know, you could have been the one who set it on fire!" Joe said angrily.

"You think *I* set it on fire?" Willy asked, raising his eyebrows. "Why would I do that? The flames might have spread and burned down the maintenance shed—including all my stuff!"

Frank ran his hands through his hair and sighed deeply. "I guess you're right. I'm sorry, Willy. Anyone could have locked me in there and started the fire." He looked at the older man. "But what were you doing here with that bulldozer?"

"I just came back from clearing that road and was going to put the 'dozer away when I saw the smoke and flames," Willy explained. "I heard you yelling, so I grabbed the fire extinguisher from the maintenance shack and doused the fire. I couldn't find the key to the lock, so I figured the bulldozer was the only way to get you out of that smoke trap."

"Thanks for getting me out of there," Frank said.

Willy shrugged. "I would have let that old shed burn down. We need a new one, anyway. I never figured anyone would be fool enough to get himself locked inside."

They turned and looked at the fire-blackened shed with the gaping hole on one side.

Suddenly, Frank remembered the map. He scrambled back through the hole and searched the shed thoroughly, but the map was nowhere to be found. It must have fallen through one of the floorboards and burned up, Frank thought. He sighed. A clue, possibly an important one, was gone forever.

"Just looking for my flashlight," Frank said as he stepped out of the shed. Joe looked at his brother quizzically.

"So now we've got a mystery fire to add to everything else," Willy grumbled. "Oh, don't think I don't know that you know all about what's been happening here," he went on, giving Frank and Joe a shrewd glance. "You're in real tight with Steve. I reckon he told you everything."

"About what?" Joe asked innocently.

"Oh, stuff missing, you know—things not being where they're supposed to be. Like the big roll of fencing wire for the vegetable garden that just disappeared. Who'd want to go and take that?"

"Anything else?" Frank asked.

"My little backpack shovel. And some felt markers I used to label stuff. They just disappeared. You think someone's got it in for me?" Willy asked, shaking his head sadly. "Well, I'd better go tell

Steve about his tool shed." He walked away, still shaking his head.

"Maybe it was spontaneous combustion that started the fire," Joe suggested. "That happens sometimes."

"Sure—right after the door 'spontaneously' locked itself." Frank stared at the shed. Then he told his brother about the map he had found. "Somewhere in there, in a heap of ashes, is the only real clue we've turned up."

The Hardys stood in silence for a moment. Both of them were thinking the same thing—that this case was going nowhere fast.

"I saw Willy, you know," Joe said finally. "He was bringing the bulldozer around the front of the lodge. I caught a glimpse of him from the office window."

He glanced over at his older brother. "It would have been almost impossible for him to start the fire, let it catch, and then get back on the bulldozer to rescue you."

"I guess that positively clears him," Frank admitted. "I've still got my doubts about him, though."

"Maybe you're right," said Joe. "But he'd never have rescued you if he was responsible for the other 'accidents,' too."

Frank nodded. "You don't really believe the fire was started by spontaneous combustion, do you?" he asked.

Joe shook his head and frowned. "There was definitely a human hand at work here. One with a match in it." He glanced at his watch. "Hey, it's lunchtime. Let's see if anyone's back from the not-so-happy hunting ground."

The Hardys walked back to the lodge. As they stepped inside, they could hear Mr. Peters complaining about his lost binoculars.

"Here they are!" he said in his gravelly voice. He picked up the little binoculars from the lost and found table. "I was helpless all morning. Couldn't see a thing without them!"

"Uh-huh. Too bad," Fletcher said as he guided the elderly birdwatcher into the dining room.

By the time Maggie brought in a big pot of steaming hot tomato soup, everyone was seated at the long table—except for Willy and the Three B's.

Mrs. Ackerly was passing Joe a plate of hot biscuits when Willy arrived and took a seat.

"So, how'd the hunting go?" the maintenance man asked, looking around the table. "See anything in the woods?"

Randall and Mallory shook their heads. So did Peters, from where he sat hunched over his soup plate.

"No luck *yet?*" Willy said in disbelief. "Maybe Brown, Buckley, and Burns think they'll do better staying out all day."

"What makes you think that?" Joe asked.

"I told them the deer don't move around much this time of day," Willy replied. "The tall one, Buckley, just acted as if he knew better. Said they'd take their chances. I thought maybe they'd seen something and didn't want to tell anyone else."

"Those men certainly keep to themselves," said Mrs. Ackerly. "I asked them what business they're in down in Providence, and you know what? They changed the subject right away." She turned to Willy. "Why, I bet they refused to tell you where they were going."

"As a matter of fact, they mentioned that they were going over to Moose Jaw Ridge," Willy replied.

Frank dropped his soup spoon on the floor. As he bent to pick it up, Joe leaned over and asked in a whisper, "What's the matter with you?"

Frank answered him in a low voice. "Remember that map I saw in the shed?"

Joe nodded.

"There were three X's on it—and one of them was Moose Jaw Ridge!"

9 Hanging in There

"What are we waiting for?" Joe whispered impatiently. "Let's get going!"

The Hardys finished their lunch quickly. As soon as they could politely leave, they excused themselves. On the way out, Frank said to Steve, "Would you mind showing us that guidebook you said you had in your office?"

"Sure," the lodge owner said. He put down his napkin, got up, and followed Frank and Joe out of the dining room.

Frank told Steve about the map he had found in the tool shed. "We have to get over to Moose Jaw Ridge as quickly as possible," Frank said. "Can you suggest the best way to do that?"

Steve nodded. "So you think there's something fishy about the Three B's?" he asked.

"Maybe," Joe said. "Or maybe it's a coincidence that they decided to go there."

"In any case, there's only one way to find out," Frank continued. "And that's for us to head there ourselves."

Steve led them to his office.

"There's no real road from here." He pointed to the map on the wall behind his desk. "But we did mark a trail with strips of yellow plastic ribbons a few months back—or rather, Willy did. You could follow that."

The Hardys thanked Steve and headed for their cabin to prepare for the hike.

"Are you ready, Joe?" asked Frank, tying up his wilderness boots.

"Ready as I'll ever be," Joe told him as he adjusted a small backpack onto his shoulders.

The brothers wound scarves around their necks, slid into their down jackets, and left the cabin.

Steve caught up with them at the point where the trail from their cabin met the main path. "I marked the way to the beginning of our trail," he said. "Stay to the right of the yellow ribbons when you reach them." He called out after the brothers as they rushed off, "And watch out for frozen patches. There could be deep water under thin ice!"

Following the map Willy had given them earlier, the Hardys had an easy enough time finding the beginning of the marked trail. As they slogged

78

through the underbrush, they kept an eye open for the yellow ribbons. They weren't that hard to follow. Willy had done a good job marking the trail.

"Willy sure knows these woods well," Frank said, as they trudged along. "Steve's lucky to have him working at the lodge. Now I feel a little guilty for suspecting him of doing anything."

"The forest is really beautiful, isn't it?" said Joe, glancing at the pines and hemlocks towering above them. Rays of sunlight shot down between the trees.

"That's weird," Frank said suddenly.

"What is?" asked Joe.

"Suddenly I don't see any yellow ribbons anywhere," Frank replied. "They just sort of stop."

Joe looked around. "You're right," he said. "I don't see any, either. So where do we go now?"

"Let's see if we can pick up any kind of a trail," Frank suggested. He glanced around. "It looks a little clearer over there, to the left."

They worked their way through the thick woods toward the clearing. When they got there, they saw that the clearing was covered with a pile of branches.

"These branches have been cut," said Frank. "Look, they're covering stumps! And here are the felled trees—they've been moved out of the way and covered with more branches."

"Well, what do you know," Joe said, staring at

the pile of branches. "There's a yellow ribbon on this one!" He pointed at one of the fallen trees.

Frank knelt by a downed log and brushed branches away to get a better look. "These trees have been cut clean through," he said. "That could explain the mysterious sound of the chainsaw during the night."

"But why would anyone want to cut trees secretly?" Joe wanted to know.

"Well, it's one way to mess up the trail," Frank replied.

"They could do that just by switching ribbons," said Joe. His eyes lit up. "Wait a minute. Maybe they have! We don't really know if we've been on the right trail for Moose Jaw Ridge."

"You're right," Frank said. "We can't trust the trail. So we'll have to figure things out ourselves." He frowned for a moment, thinking. "That X was on the top right side of the map. That means the northeast."

He squinted up at the sun, trying to estimate its position in the sky. "This time of year, the sun sets more to the northwest than plain west," he said.

"And with those shadows falling behind us this time of day, we should keep heading toward the sun, and a little to the right."

They set off through the woods once again.

Several minutes later, they came to a clear path. "I bet we're on the right trail now," Joe said.

80

Frank, however, was looking in another direction. "You may be right," he said. "But I see a yellow ribbon over there."

With Frank in the lead, the Hardys worked their way over toward the tree with the yellow ribbon. As they walked, dead and broken branches crackled and popped under their feet.

"Don't move!" Joe suddenly shouted.

"Huh?" asked Frank, stopping short. "What's wrong?"

"Look in front of you, underneath those branches," Joe ordered.

Frank peered down at the pile of branches. Underneath the pile, barely visible, was the dark, gleaming surface of an iced-over pond.

"Those branches didn't fall on the pond by accident," Frank said. "They're too carefully arranged. Someone put them there deliberately!"

"Remember what Steve told us about deep water under thin ice?" asked Joe. He picked up a large, heavy rock and heaved it through an opening in the pile of branches.

There was a loud cracking sound, followed by an ugly gurgle as the stone sank beneath the icy surface.

"That would have been pretty chilly," Frank said, taking a long look at the foiled trap. "And one dip was enough for today."

They moved off in the opposite direction, toward the clearing in the woods that Joe had discovered.

"We'd better get a move on," Frank said. "We lost a lot of time on that false trail."

Using a thick piece of a branch to bushwhack their way through the forest, they trudged on, picking up the pace whenever the trail opened up.

They reached a wide, open stretch of trail, and Joe started to jog ahead of his brother.

"What do you think this is, a marathon?" Frank shouted, as he surged forward to catch up to Joe.

Ahead of them, the trees opened up into an even wider clearing. Joe sped up and Frank pounded after him.

As Joe approached the edge of the clearing, he shouted, "And it's Joe Hardy in the lead. It looks like Hardy will break the tape first. Yes, folks, Joe Hardy is the winner!"

"Forget it!" Frank yelled, as he caught up to his brother. "We're breaking this tape to—"

He never finished the sentence.

There was a click as both Hardys tripped over an invisible wire and a loud *thwang!* echoed through the stillness of the forest.

A second later, the Hardy brothers found themselves bound up in wire mesh—and soaring high into the air.

10 Friends to the Rescue

The mesh trap spun and swung wildly in the air. Frank and Joe became dizzier and dizzier.

Finally, the trap stopped spinning around. The Hardys breathed sighs of relief. Then they began to check out their surroundings.

"Treetops! That's all I can see," said Joe, peering through the wire.

Squashed up next to him, Frank added, "And birds. It's as if we were in some giant bird cage."

"It must have been a kind of spring trap connected to some sort of pulley," said Joe, frowning. "But you don't use that for deer."

"Somehow, I don't think this trap was meant for deer," Frank said grimly. He pressed against the crossed wires, trying to find a weak link or some way to climb out. There was none.

"Now I know how a parrot feels. Or a canary," Joe said, as he worked at the mesh with his hand. The wire bent fairly easily, and soon Joe made an opening large enough for his arm. He reached through the opening and flapped his hand in the breeze.

He nodded at a flock of birds in the distance. "Those geese over there are lucky. They can fly."

"They're probably buzzards, just waiting to peck away at us when we starve to death up here," Frank said glumly.

Joe gave his brother a look, then turned back to stare into the sky. "One of them can't seem to wait," he said. "It's breaking away from the flock."

Frank peered through the wire. "Yeah, and it's getting closer," he said. "I can hear it. I didn't know geese made buzzing noises." He listened more carefully. "Wait a minute, that's not a bird sound!" he shouted above the noise. "It's an engine!"

"And that's no bird," Joe added. "It's a helicopter! Think the pilot will be able to see us?"

"He might not," Frank said. "Wiggle! Move! We have to attract his attention."

"Wait a second! I've got it," cried Joe. He yanked his arm back into the cage, then fumbled around until he managed to reach into his pocket and pull out Iola's bright red scarf. Squeezing his arm back through the wires, he flapped the scarf wildly in the air.

"Come on," Joe muttered between clenched teeth. "Get the signal and get over here!"

Joe's arm was beginning to ache, but he continued to wave the scarf. Just when he thought his arm was about to drop off, Frank shouted, "They're heading in our direction! They've seen us!"

The sound of the engine grew louder as the helicopter came closer. Soon it was hovering just above the clearing. Then it landed gently on the ground.

The rotors slowly stopped spinning. Then three young men got out of the chopper. One of them, a heavyset young man, looked up. "Don't you guys have anything better to do than hang around all day?" he called up to Frank and Joe.

"I can't believe it!" Joe gasped. "It's Chet. And I can see Biff, too."

"Just get us out of here," Frank yelled down.

The Hardys waited impatiently. Finally, they felt themselves being lowered. When they were on the ground, the pilot went to work on the mesh with a pair of wire clippers.

Chet Morton and Biff Hooper stood there smiling at them.

"What took you guys so long?" Frank asked jokingly.

Biff, who was tall and muscular, stared at him. Then he looked at Chet. "Nice, real nice," he said. "That's all the thanks we get for saving their lives."

Chet just shook his head. "And for this I sold my ticket to a pro football game."

"Okay, okay," Frank said, laughing. "Thanks, you guys. We're really glad you showed up, believe me."

The pilot had snipped a hole big enough for Frank and Joe to climb out. The brothers gratefully stepped onto the ground.

Then the five of them climbed into the chopper. The pilot revved up his engine.

"Would you mind circling over and around Moose Jaw Ridge?" Frank asked the pilot, after they had taken off.

The chopper operator shrugged and set the course. About five minutes later, the pilot said, "We're passing over Moose Jaw Ridge now."

Frank and Joe peered out the window.

"Just a huge ridge of trees," Joe said. "And there's no sign of those guys."

"I guess we lost too much time getting here," Frank said. "We may as well head for the lodge now." He turned to Chet and Biff. "I guess I should ask how you guys happened to be passing by. We didn't expect you till tomorrow."

"It's your dad—he's amazing," Chet said. "When we told him that we'd heard from you, he

86

insisted we leave right away and not wait to get the early plane to Portland tomorrow morning."

"Right," said Biff. "He called some old pal of his who runs a commuter service with old army helicopters, and the next thing we knew, we were on this chopper."

As they headed back toward the lodge, Frank and Joe filled Chet and Biff in on the situation at Lakeside Lodge. They also gave them a rundown on the guests.

"By the way, we're not supposed to know you guys," Frank said. "We'd better not all arrive together."

He asked the pilot to let him and Joe off on the other side of a ridge to the north of the lodge. They could easily hike back from there.

The pilot found a clearing and landed. Frank and Joe thanked him for his help and jumped out of the chopper. They waved to Chet and Biff and set off toward the lodge. The sun was setting, so the Hardys walked quickly. Neither of them wanted to be hiking in the dark forest.

When the Hardys got back to the lodge, Chet and Biff were already seated around the roaring blaze in the living room, sipping steaming hot cocoa from mugs.

Frank and Joe shrugged off their down jackets and headed into the kitchen for some cocoa, too.

When they returned to the living room, Chet was

just beginning a story about his supposed adventures on safari in Africa.

Frank and Joe glanced at each other. Joe rolled his eyes.

Chet's audience, the three businessmen from Providence, didn't seem very interested in Chet's story.

"How long do we have to wait for dinner, anyhow?" Mr. Buckley complained.

"You must be pretty hungry after a full day out in the woods," Frank said.

"With no lunch," Joe added.

"Unless there's a restaurant out there at Moose Jaw Ridge," Frank said. He waited to see their reactions.

"Very funny!" snapped Mr. Brown.

"Besides, we never went there," Mr. Burns put in nervously. "It was too far. We came back right after . . . after lunch."

"Well, Maggie's dinner will make up for your missed lunch," Joe said. Then he introduced himself and his brother to the "newcomers," Chet and Biff, and asked whether they had ever been to Maine.

Chet launched into a story of his hiking adventures in the Canadian Rockies. Biff quickly suggested they go and clean up before dinner and herded his friend out of the living room.

Dinner was quiet, except for Chet's made-up

88

stories about his various hiking triumphs. Biff managed to change the subject each time Chet got started.

After all the guests had gone off to their cabins or bedrooms, Steve sat in the living room with the Hardys, Chet, and Biff over coffee.

"It's really unusual for any of the guests to go this long without bagging at least one deer," he said. "The area is so overcrowded you can hardly miss."

He shook his head. "And if the hunters don't put them down, a lot of deer just won't make it through the winter. There's not enough vegetation and cleared land for them to feed. Without food, they can't protect themselves from predators." He got up from the sofa. "Well, I've got some work to do in the office. See you tomorrow." He left the room.

Frank turned to Chet. "You really don't have to overdo your hiking experience," he told his friend.

"Right," Joe said. "*We* know your idea of a hike is to walk to the refrigerator during TV commercials for a snack, but the guests here don't know that."

"Wise guy," said Chet. "Well, how about taking a hike to our room to look at the information your dad sent you."

"What are you talking about?" asked Frank.

"What information?" asked Joe.

"You'll see," Chet said smugly.

The four of them headed to Chet and Biff's room at the far end of the lodge. When they got there,

Chet reached into his suitcase and took out a large manila envelope.

"Your father's done some research for you," he said.

"Some friends down at the *Bayport Times* dug this out of their morgue for him." Biff took the folder, opened it, and spread a pile of photocopies of newspaper clippings on the bed.

"Wow, the lodge looks really run-down in this photo," said Joe.

"The clippings go back thirteen years," Chet said with a yawn. "I looked at them on the plane."

"They're mostly about the robbery," said Frank, reading. "It gives the names of the robbers—Hank Jones, Sam Green, Ace Birdwell, and Matt Graham."

"There's a few about the trial," said Joe. "The crooks got thirteen years in jail apiece."

"Here's one dated just a few months ago," said Frank.

"What's it say?" Biff asked.

"It says that the three robbers who were caught and convicted were recently released from the federal penitentiary on parole." He looked up at his brother, an excited expression on his face. "And you'll never guess where the penitentiary is."

"Where?" Joe asked.

Frank gave them a huge grin and said, "Providence!"

11 Gray Day

Biff leaned forward. "Is there anything else?" he asked excitedly. "Any pictures of these guys?"

Joe and Frank quickly riffled through the photocopies.

"Here's an old one taken outside the trial." Frank squinted as he held up one clipping dated the thirteenth of the month. "But it's so old and blurry, you can't really tell anything from it."

"There have to be some new pictures around somewhere," Joe said. Suddenly his eyes lit up. "And I know just the person who'd have them— Len Randall!"

"Right," Frank said. "Let's see if he and Mallory are in their cabin."

The Hardys said good night to Biff, since Chet was already fast asleep on his bed, and crept out of

91

the lodge. They quickly made their way to the cabin shared by Len Randall and Mike Mallory.

Frank knocked on the door. It was opened almost immediately by Randall.

"Guys, I can't help you," Randall said after Frank explained why they were there.

"Give us a break," Joe said. "We just want to take a quick look. You know, for our school project."

The reporter shrugged his shoulders. "Even if I wanted to, I couldn't," he said. "The stupid thing has disappeared."

"What?" Joe exclaimed.

"Yup, must have happened while I was scouting around this morning," said Randall. Then he added, "But I don't care. I've got a bigger story."

It took a lot of pleading, but the Hardys managed to worm it out of him.

"A UFO!" Randall said breathlessly.

As the Hardys' eyebrows shot up, he nodded vigorously. "I sighted it myself, just as the sun was starting to go down," he said. "Mike and I were coming back from that trail leading over the ridge when I heard the whine of an engine way off in the distance. Over those tall pines, I saw a glowing red object circle, then land in a clearing. Mike got a great picture of it."

"You saw a helicopter, Len," Joe said flatly. "A plain, ordinary chopper reflected in the sunset."

Randall smiled at them slyly. "Maybe to *you* it was a chopper. To my readers, it'll be a UFO. It's the perfect story," he added gleefully. "Think of the headline!"

"I know one headline no one would believe," Joe said as they walked away from Randall and Mallory's cabin.

"What's that?" Frank asked.

" 'Len Randall Tells the Truth.' "

Frank laughed and shook his head. "That's all Steve needs—people up here looking for UFOs!"

"Speaking of Steve," said Joe, "let's see if he can tell us any more about the Three B's."

Frank nodded. "They're our prime suspects now."

When they got to the office, they saw that Steve was on the phone.

"Look, we're getting dangerously low," he was saying into the receiver. "We need to have more generator fuel or we'll run out of power. Do you know what that means out here? When? You can't make it any sooner?" He sighed. "All right, we'll just have to cut down till then."

He hung up the phone.

"Can't get an emergency shipment till sometime tomorrow at the earliest," he told the boys. "I'd better let everyone know we'll have to conserve power. In fact, I think I'll turn off the generator tonight." He made a note on the desk pad, then sat back in his seat. "Now, what's up, guys? Any developments?"

Frank and Joe told him what they'd discovered about the robbers from Fenton's clippings and their suspicions about Burns, Brown, and Buckley. "Those may not be their real names. Can you tell us anything about their reservations or registration?" Frank asked Steve. "Maybe the way they made them would give us something to go on."

Steve shook his head. "They just called and said they'd like to come up. I think they claimed they heard about the lodge from a friend."

"What about their credit cards?" Joe asked. "We could have Dad check them out through them."

"Can't help you there," Steve said. "They paid cash in advance for the full week. Nice, crisp bills."

Discouraged, the Hardys left Steve's office and headed up to Chet and Biff's room.

They knocked on the door, then opened it a crack.

They saw Biff doing push-ups on the floor. Chet was sprawled out dozing on the bed with a copy of James Fenimore Cooper's *The Deerslayer* tented over his eyes.

"Well, at least he woke up long enough to decide what book to read," Joe commented.

Frank and Joe looked at each other and nodded.

There was no real reason to disturb either of them right now. They just told Biff that they'd see him at breakfast and left.

"Tomorrow, we'll split up and follow good old Burnsie, Buckley, and Brownie," said Joe, as they headed back to their cabin. "I'm convinced they're up here after that loot. But I can't figure out why they just don't go and get it. Why go to all this trouble with phony paths and traps and ghosts?"

"Some of it falls into place," Frank said. "I mean, the missing wire was for the trap, and the shovel had to be for digging. But you're right. How does digging for stolen money fit in with everything else that's been going on here?"

"I give up," Joe said, yawning. "Let's just sleep on it. Tomorrow, you take one, I'll take another, and we'll get Chet and Biff to tail the third. That ought to turn up something."

The weather the next morning put a kink on the Hardys' plan. A steady torrent of sleet and freezing rain came down in sheets.

"Looks like we're stuck in here today," said Mrs. Ackerly, sipping tea near the fire in the living room. Her husband whistled happily as he sat next to her, doing a crossword puzzle. Randall and Mallory and Peters and Fletcher had gone back to their cabins right after breakfast.

95

"Might as well oil up some of the machines," said Willy. He bundled up and headed off to the maintenance shack.

Frank and Joe sat at a bridge table playing cards with Chet and Biff. "Here come the Three B's," Chet murmured as he shuffled the cards for another game of Hearts.

Carrying mugs of coffee, the three from Providence filed in from the dining room. They wandered around the living room, picking up magazines, staring at them, then dropping them back in the rack or on the end tables.

"Let's see if we can get those guys over here," Biff muttered. He took the deck of cards from Chet.

"Hey," he said loudly, "anyone want to play Concentration?"

He shuffled the cards, then laid them all out on the table, facedown.

Chet went first. He picked up the two of clubs and then the seven of spades. Then he turned them back down right where they were.

Frank went next. He picked up the ace of diamonds and the jack of hearts. He turned them back down.

Joe picked up the two of clubs.

"Great!" he crowed. "Now let's see if I can remember where that seven of spades was."

He picked up a card, but it was the three of diamonds.

Biff quickly snapped up the ace of diamonds that Frank had turned over and then the three of diamonds.

"One to nothing," Biff announced.

Brown, Buckley, and Burns had been watching the game with interest.

Brown turned to Buckley and said, "Hey, want to give it a try? How about you, Burnsie?"

"Might as well," answered the usually silent Burns. "I'll go get some more cards. There's a deck in my room."

Chet and Biff began to score heavily against both Frank and Joe. Somehow, the Hardys just couldn't seem to keep their minds on the game.

Brown and Buckley hovered over the table and kept up a running comment on the game. They didn't seem to notice that it had been a long time since Burns had gone for the deck of cards.

But Frank did.

Claiming he wanted to get a drink of water, he left the living room after his turn, telling Joe to take an extra shot if he wasn't back in time for his next one.

He crept upstairs along the corridor to the guest bedrooms. There was a door open on one side.

Frank tiptoed to the open door. He quickly discovered that he hadn't needed to sneak around.

Lying across the floor, in front of the open doorway, was the unconscious form of Mr. Burns.

97

Frank bent over and tapped the man lightly on the cheek.

"Mr. Burns! Mr. Burns!" he called.

The man on the floor blinked his eyes open and started to lift his head.

"What happened?" Frank asked.

Burns looked at Joe, his eyes filled with terror. "He . . . he said 'thirteen,'" Burns whispered.

"Who said thirteen?" Frank asked.

"A . . . a ghost," whispered Burns.

Then he fainted again.

12 A Sudden Flash

Frank stared at Burns for a second, then hurried into the bathroom. He soaked a small hand towel with cold water and rushed back to the collapsed Burns.

Frank pressed the cold towel to Burns's forehead. The shock of the cold water brought the short businessman around again. He opened his eyes, glanced around fearfully, then focused on Frank. "Wha—what are you doing here?"

"I heard a thump, came to check it out, and found you on the floor. Are you okay?"

"Oh—sure. Sure, I'm fine." Burns sat up, still holding the towel to his head. "I—um—must have slipped."

"The first time you came around, you mentioned

99

something about the number thirteen and a ghost," Frank told him.

Burns went pale and his washed-out blue eyes darted back and forth nervously. "I didn't think—I mean, I must have been a little delirious."

He struggled to his feet, walked unsteadily to the bed, and sat down. Then he looked up at Frank and squinted. "Look, kid, thanks for helping me out— but do me a favor, okay? Don't mention this to anyone. If Brown and Buckley found out about this, they'd never let me live it down."

Just then, Buckley and Brown stomped into the room with Biff, Chet, and Joe trailing behind. They all stared at the sight of Burns sitting on the bed, dabbing his forehead with the damp towel, while Frank loomed over him.

"What's going on here?" yelled Buckley.

"Burnsie, are you okay?" cried Brown, rushing over to his friend.

Burns yanked away the wet towel and looked up at his companions. His face was still ashen.

"I'm—I'm all right, now," he said, scowling. "Just leave me alone!"

"What happened?" asked Mr. Buckley. He turned to Frank, his eyes narrowing with suspicion. "And what are you doing up here?"

"I heard a noise," Frank replied. "A thud. So I came up to see what happened. Your buddy here had fainted. Then he came to for a minute and said he saw—"

Burns glared at Frank, his face beginning to return to its normal red.

"I don't know what you're talking about," Mr. Burns snapped. "I—I didn't see anything."

The tall, thin Buckley gave the Hardys and Chet and Biff a hard look. "Why don't you guys go back to your game," he said, ushering them toward the door. "We'll look after our pal here."

As soon as the Hardys and Chet and Biff were out of the room, Buckley closed the door and locked it.

"I guess the show's over," Joe said. He looked at his brother curiously. "What did Burns say, Frank?"

"Let's talk about it in Chet and Biff's room," Frank whispered, glancing at the closed door to Burns's room.

After they had stepped into Chet and Biff's room, Frank said, "I can't figure out what that fainting scene was all about."

"It's hard to believe a tough-looking guy like Burns fainted," Biff said. "I thought you'd gotten into a fight with him or something."

Frank shook his head. "He was already on the floor when I found him. When he came to, he said he'd seen a ghost who mentioned the number thirteen, and then he fainted again."

101

"I don't get it," Joe said.

"That makes two of us," Frank replied with a grimace. "If those phony businessmen are the crooks, then who's the ghost?"

"Wait a minute," Joe said suddenly. "There were four bandits involved in the robbery. Suppose number four is still on the loose?"

"Thirteen," Frank said thoughtfully. "The robbery was thirteen years ago, they got a sentence of thirteen years—and the date the three stood trial was on the thirteenth of the month!"

"Right!" said Joe, his eyes lighting up. "Whoever pulled this stunt had to know old Burnsie—and know how superstitious he is about the number thirteen. This was a good try at frightening him away."

"Especially if it was someone he recognized— and thought was dead," Biff suggested.

Just then, Chet, who had been working his way through a midmorning snack of potato chips, began to mumble.

"Swallow," Joe commanded.

Chet gulped down the remains of his snack, brushed the crumbs away from his mouth, and announced clearly: "That's probably why they sounded so uptight when I went by that room on the way down to breakfast."

"You didn't tell us that!" Joe said excitedly. "Did you hear anything? Anything clear enough?"

"Well," Chet admitted, "they were talking real low. Whispering, really. But one of them—Brown, I think—got excited and cried something like 'Really go for it now!' The other guys shut him up pretty quickly."

"I wish we had a recent picture of the robbers," Frank said. "Or more information about them getting out on parole. It would be nice to have something that positively tied those three to the bank robbery."

"Why don't we call Dad and see if he can get us anything?" Joe suggested.

"He's bound to know someone somewhere who can dig it up," Biff added.

Frank nodded. "That's a good idea."

"Look," Chet said, pointing to the window. "The storm's over." A bright swath of sunshine had suddenly burst in through the window.

"That means everyone will probably be hitting the trail," Frank said. "Chet, Biff, why don't you tail the Three B's. We'll hang around until everyone leaves, then we'll make that call to Dad. We'll catch up with you later."

The lodge was a hive of activity. Mrs. Ackerly rushed out of the kitchen with a thermos of coffee.

"Come on, Arthur," she said briskly. "This is going to be our lucky day. I can feel it in my bones."

From the front porch of the lodge, the brothers saw Randall and Mallory heading off on the trail leading to the ridge. Mr. Peters trudged slowly after Mr. Fletcher, who was carrying a large knapsack on his back.

The three men from Providence came rushing down the stairs. They started getting into the heavy-duty boots they'd left by the front door.

On her way out Mrs. Ackerly stopped by the Three B's. "You men look as if you're getting ready for a war, instead of hunting," she said with a big smile. "By the way, do you have any place special in mind? Just for safety's sake," she added hurriedly. "We wouldn't want to find ourselves walking into your aim—or you walking into ours, would we, Arthur?"

Mr. Buckley mumbled something about trying their luck out at Horn Point.

Frank announced loudly to Joe, "Too bad we have to work on our story today. Looks like we'll miss out on some good hiking."

"Right," Joe said, picking up the cue. "I really hate having to do homework on vacation."

As the three businessmen finished lacing up their boots, Chet and Biff pounded down the stairs. They were both wearing brand-new jeans, ragg sweaters and socks, new hiking boots, down jackets, and broad-brimmed felt hats.

"They look like an ad for L. L. Bean," Joe whispered to Frank.

Chet and Biff nodded slightly at the Hardys as they headed out the door.

The Hardys waited as patiently as possible until everyone was gone. Then Frank turned to Joe.

"I just remembered another spot marked by one of those X's on the map. Horn Point. It hit me as soon as Buckley mentioned the name. After we call Dad, we can take that new trail Willy cleared and get there in half the time it's going to take them."

They headed for the lodge office.

It was quiet and strangely peaceful inside the lodge. In the distance, they could hear the hum of the vacuum cleaner. From the kitchen came the spicy scent of apple and cinnamon.

Steve's office was deserted.

"He said it was okay to use his phone anytime," said Joe. "Go ahead, you dial."

He strolled back and forth in front of the window that faced the road leading to the cabins as Frank picked up the phone.

"I think I'm going to call person-to-person to make sure Dad's there," Frank said. "Hello, operator. Yes, this is a person-to-person call for Fenton Hardy." He gave her the number. "Yes, I'll wait."

After a few moments he said, "Hello, Dad? I need you to—"

The blast of a shotgun cut him off in midsentence.

105

13 The Trail Widens

Clutching the phone, Frank ducked back from the open window. Joe had already dropped to the floor. A second later, they heard a crash.

The Hardys got up slowly and crept toward the window. Cautiously, they opened it and looked outside.

A tangled mass of metal and wire lay on the ground. At the top of the telephone pole, a few feet away, was an empty space where the brackets that supported the telephone's transformer had been.

The door slammed open as Steve came running into the office.

"What happened?" he gasped.

"Somebody prefers communicating with a shotgun rather than a phone," Frank said grimly, point-

106

ing to the telephone pole. "So he—or she— decided to take out the transformer. Don't plan on making any calls today."

Steve shut his eyes and groaned. "I can't believe this. We're totally cut off now. The radio's been down since yesterday. Willy went to work on it and found parts missing. And his supply of spares was gone, too, so he still can't fix it."

Joe gave a low whistle. "Someone definitely doesn't want us to make contact with the outside world."

Frank leaned out the window and stared up at the telephone pole. "That had to be an incredible shot. I was standing right near the window and didn't see anybody in the clear. It had to come from some distance."

"Mrs. Ackerly?" suggested Joe.

"Could be," Frank said with a nod. "But just because she was a whiz at darts doesn't mean she's Annie Oakley. Remember, she hasn't bagged a deer the whole time she's been here."

"I'm going to try a little climb to the top of that pole," Joe said. "Maybe I'll be able to see something from there."

"But the transformer was on top—" Steve started to say.

"And when you get there, anybody who's watching will see *you*," Frank pointed out. "You'd be a perfect target."

"I still think I should check it out," Joe insisted stubbornly.

The Hardys and Steve headed outside. Joe stepped up on the pole and began to climb. He was careful to step on the little footholds that ran all the way up the pole.

When he reached the top, his suspicions were rewarded. A close-up look at the telephone pole revealed a thin wire running up to the top.

"Let's see where this goes," said Frank. He crawled on his hands and knees into the bushes along the path.

The thin wire, half-buried under surface dirt, led to a small black metal box full of chips, wires, and electronic parts. There was a large switch on the front of the box.

Frank held up the box. "How do you like this?"

"What is it?" Steve asked.

"It looks like some kind of homemade remote control," said Frank. "This is how the explosion was triggered—with an explosive device, not a shotgun!"

"That takes Mrs. Ackerly out of the spotlight," Joe said. "Unless she's an electronics expert. What about the Three B's?"

"Maybe they split up and one of them came back to stage the blast," Frank said. "But why? And how did anyone know we were making a phone

108

call? We didn't really discuss it until after everyone left."

Joe's face wore a grim expression. "I think maybe we overlooked the first thing we should have checked."

"I think you're right," Frank said.

The Hardys raced back into the lodge and Steve's office, the lodge owner following close behind.

While Joe checked around the room, Frank picked up the phone and unscrewed the mouthpiece. He pulled out a tiny, round metal disc.

"A bug! This phone's been bugged right from the start!"

"But where's the equipment, their receiver?" asked Steve.

"It could be anywhere." Frank sighed as he waved a hand at the forest outside the window. "There are just too many places to hide things out there."

"Including the loot," Joe said. "If it's the Three B's, I'm sure that's what they're after, but . . ."

"But what?" Steve asked.

"Why are they going to so much trouble, hanging around and making a big production out of it? Why don't they just dig it up and leave?" Frank finished his brother's question.

"Maybe it's time we asked them that question," said Joe. "Face-to-face."

"Let's see how fast we can get ourselves to Horn Point," Frank said. "Steve, is the ATV working?"

The lodge owner nodded. "It's about the only thing that *is* working around here."

Joe started for the door. "Then let's go!"

"Wait a minute," Steve called after them. "It's only meant to carry one person."

"We'll improvise," Joe shouted back.

Fifteen minutes later, the Hardy brothers were on an incline that was part of the trail to Horn Point. But with two of them on the ATV, they couldn't accelerate it to full speed, in spite of Joe's best efforts to rev it up.

"I guess this is what Steve meant when he warned us that the ATV should carry only one person," Joe said with a sigh.

"Look, this is a mistake," Frank said. "This thing will get us there faster if only one of us rides. You handle it best, so why don't you drive on just to the south of Horn Point? We both have maps, so we shouldn't get lost. You can keep an eye out for the Three B's. If you're lucky, you'll bump into Chet and Biff, too."

"What about you?" Joe asked.

Frank shrugged. "I'll follow on foot. Just don't confront those guys if you find them before I get there."

"You're sure you want to walk?" Joe asked skeptically.

110

"I'm sure," Frank urged. "Here, take some of my gear."

He unloaded his own daypack and strapped it onto Joe's back. "Now get going," he shouted.

After Joe had ridden off, Frank jogged along the trail. He scanned the woods for any signs of a quicker way to get to Horn Point. Every once in a while, he consulted the map to check the distance to Horn Point.

Off to one side, the brush thinned a little, and he noticed a small path that looked as though it had been cut recently. He decided to investigate, in case it turned out to be a shortcut. About ten feet along the path, however, he came upon a clump of fresh branches.

Remembering the camouflaged ice pond, he grabbed a stick and carefully stirred through the branches. One by one they fell off the pile until Frank could see the object buried underneath.

The steely jaws of a heavy metal bear trap gaped at him.

Frank's stomach did a flip-flop as he stared at the deadly trap. He took a deep breath and let it out slowly. "I'd better stick with the main trail," he murmured.

Then another thought hit him. If the shortcut had been booby-trapped, what about the main road?

Worried for Joe, Frank turned around to

111

backtrack—and nearly leapt back into the jaws of the trap behind him.

A huge, dark form was blocking the trail Frank had used. The older Hardy brother gasped.

He was face-to-face with an uncaged, untamed, and hungry-looking bear!

14 Close Encounters with the Animal Kingdom

The enormous, snuffling bear moved slowly but steadily toward Frank. The older Hardy brother found himself staring into the animal's face. Then the bear stopped. Its beady brown eyes looked around, and its mouth opened, revealing long, sharp teeth.

Frank wanted to run, but he was frozen to the spot. Any sudden move, he knew, might make the bear charge him.

The bear lumbered forward again. It was getting closer and closer.

Suddenly, the revving of an engine in overdrive

caught the bear's attention. The sound turned the bear away from Frank. In a moment, the huge beast was crashing off through the brush in the opposite direction.

With a whirl of dust, Joe pulled up the ATV next to his wide-eyed older brother.

"I don't know what made you decide to come back," Frank said in a relieved tone, "but I really am glad you did."

"You can thank Biff for that," Joe said. "I met him a couple of miles up the road. He was excited about something. Turned out he'd just caught a glimpse of a big brown bear a little ways back— heading right where I'd left you." Joe grinned at his brother. "Biff couldn't say whether or not the bear had eaten lunch yet, so I figured I'd better see if you were on the menu."

"He was starting to lick his chops just as you pulled up," Frank said. "What was Biff doing all by himself, anyhow?"

Joe rolled his eyes. "I'll let him give his own report," he said. He glanced over his shoulder. "Unless the bear's changed his mind and come back, that sounds like Biff crashing toward us."

In a few moments the Hardys' friend jogged into the clearing.

"Whew!" puffed Biff, a little winded from his run down the trail. "They say it's harder to hit a moving target, and I'm not taking any chances."

114

"What happened?" Frank asked, after he had filled Biff in on the encounter with the bear. "Where's Chet? Why aren't the two of you keeping an eye on the boys from Providence?"

"Whoa!" Biff said, holding up his hand. "Slow down. First of all, those guys are pretty slick. We weren't out in the woods more than twenty minutes before they gave us the slip. And that's in spite of them wearing red coats!"

Joe shook his head. "You had to follow three not-so-young guys who spent the past couple of years in jail. What was the problem? Were they too fast for the two of you?"

"Well, Chet had a little trouble keeping up," Biff admitted. "But they faked me out, too. As soon as they were in the deep woods, they split up and went in three directions—at least it looked that way. Then the guy I was following, Buckley, doubled back—I found that out when he fired a few shots in my direction."

"He shot right at you?" Frank asked, raising his eyebrows.

"Not exactly. But close enough to make me want to keep clear of him," Biff replied. "I tried to hitch up with Chet again, and that's when I got a glimpse of the bear. And then Joe pulled up on the ATV."

"Seems to me we'd better find Chet before he gets into trouble," Frank suggested. "On foot," he added, looking at Joe, who was still seated in the ATV.

"You mean I'm going to have to walk?" Joe asked, rolling his eyes. "Give me a break!"

Frank grinned at him. "Well, I think we should keep together. Besides, we don't want to run out of gas." He patted the ATV with his hand. "We may need this thing later."

Frank took a last look at the bear trap. "When we get back to the lodge, I'll ask Steve to remove this little toy," he said. "Someone might get caught in it."

They started off down the trail. The path became narrower as they trudged their way through the dense forest, then it opened up again.

Biff was the first to spot someone—but it wasn't Chet. Instead, as the Hardys and Biff got close, they recognized the journalistic team of Randall and Mallory.

"Hunting for more phony stories, I bet," Joe said disgustedly.

"Hi, guys," Randall said brightly. Mallory smiled at them, then continued to adjust the telephoto lens on his camera.

"You two out here looking for Bigfoot?" Joe asked sarcastically.

Randall whirled around. "Bigfoot? Where? Did you see him?"

Joe just shook his head and sighed.

"Anyway, we *did* see something," Randall said mysteriously.

"Too bad you only get one good shot at something like that," Mallory said sadly.

"You missed a great shot, huh?" said Biff.

"I'll say." Mallory patted his camera. "This baby was loaded and ready to go, too."

"So what did you see?" Joe asked impatiently. "And don't say it was a UFO!"

Randall and Mallory looked at each other. "Well, I guess we can tell you," Randall said. "It was a huge buck."

"But it ran away before I could get a shot of it."

"So we figured we'd better get back on the main trail to look for other interesting game," said Randall. "We saw someone headed this way and thought he might lead us to something."

"You're sure it was a 'he'?" Frank asked. "Which direction did he take?"

Before Randall or Mallory could reply, a familiar voice called out, "Halloooo!"

"Was it one of the Ackerlys you saw?" Frank asked Randall and Malloy.

The journalists shook their heads.

Just then, a crashing of underbrush signaled the arrival of the Ackerlys.

"Well, hello, boys," Mrs. Ackerly said. "Fancy meeting you here."

"This looks like a hunting convention," Mr. Ackerly said with a smile. "All we need now is something to shoot at."

"Quiet!" Mallory snapped suddenly. He was staring through the telephoto lens.

Immediately the group fell silent.

"Did you hear it?" the lanky photographer whispered softly. "It's back!"

They stood still and waited.

Then the silence was broken by a trumpeting bellow in the distance. It was unlike any animal sound any of them had heard near Lakeside Lodge.

"That's a moose call," Mr. Ackerly said. "I've heard it on nature programs."

"It's coming from over in that direction," Randall whispered, pointing north.

The group started off quietly down the trail. Mallory scanned the woods through his camera lens.

As they approached a clearing Frank whispered to Joe, "Wait till Chet finds out we've seen a moose and he's missed it."

Joe nodded. Then he took out his binoculars and peered through them all around the clearing. Suddenly, he gasped in surprise and fear.

"What's wrong?" Frank asked.

Joe handed Frank the binoculars. The older Hardy looked through them and gasped, too.

Within the circle of his vision was a terrible sight. Chet was tied to the trunk of a tree and gagged. His eyes were wide with terror as he stared at a six-point buck standing inches away from him.

15 Unmasking an Alias

The group crept closer to the clearing. Soon they could see Chet and the buck distinctly, without the help of binoculars.

"Now, *that* is what I call a trophy!" Mrs. Ackerly whispered as she gazed at the buck.

The prize buck seemed to be angry at the strange creature attached to the tree. The deer came forward. Chet's eyes were almost popping out of his head.

The buck began to scratch at the tree with its antlers. Chet tried to shrink away from the rack of pointed antlers, but he had nowhere to go.

"We have to save Chet," Frank said softly to the group.

"Wait!" Mrs. Ackerly whispered. "I want that buck!"

"Are you sure you can get a decent shot?" asked her husband.

"I've got a long-range rifle," she reminded him.

"The deer is too close to Chet," Biff objected. "If you miss the deer, you may hit him."

"All right," Mrs. Ackerly said. "We'll all sneak up closer. I'm sure some noise is bound to startle the buck. When it moves a safe distance away, I'll take my shot."

They carefully edged their way closer to the clearing.

Frank was surprised how near they got before the buck picked up their scent—or sound.

It lifted its head and turned its magnificent rack of antlers in their direction for an instant. Then the beautiful animal took off into the woods.

A split second later, a thunderous blast ripped through the silence.

"Did you get him?" Mr. Ackerly asked his wife.

"I didn't fire that shot!" she exclaimed.

"Well, then, who did?" asked Randall as they all rushed toward Chet.

His question was answered as three men in red vests burst out of the underbrush and ran toward them.

"It's Buckley, Brown, and Burns!" cried Joe. "Those guys have a lot of nerve!"

As the three businessmen came closer, the Hardys and the others could hear them arguing.

"I *told* you I was going to take a shot," said Brown.

"But it was getting away," protested Buckley.

"I had the best position," put in Burns.

"Well, we missed him," said Brown.

Frank and Joe looked at each other and smiled. In their hearts, they were glad that the buck had managed to escape.

Meanwhile, Biff had untied Chet. The heavyset teen had slumped to the ground in a dead faint.

"Out cold," Frank said. He opened his canteen and sprinkled some cold water on Chet's forehead. Chet opened his eyes and blinked. "I'm alive!" he exclaimed. "Thanks, guys." He stumbled to his feet and took a deep breath.

"How'd you get into a mess like this?" Biff asked.

Chet stomped up and down to get the circulation flowing in his legs.

"I saw a pair of suspicious individuals with hats pulled down low over their heads slinking along through the wilderness," he began dramatically.

Joe rolled his eyes. "Oh, boy. Here we go, guys."

As Chet went on, he sounded like a combination of the Mighty Hunter and the Great Detective.

". . . Anyway, after trailing these characters for some time, somehow they realized I was on their trail. . . ."

"He probably tripped over himself," Joe whispered.

"Then they attacked me, using some *trick.*"

"So, they spotted you and then grabbed you, is that what you're trying to say?" Biff asked.

Chet nodded. "It's too bad I didn't see them double back and creep up behind me."

"Were they wearing red vests?" Joe asked in a low voice, nodding in the direction of the Three B's, who were off to one side of the clearing, still arguing with one another.

Chet shook his head. "One of the men was kind of heavyset, though."

"I think we can figure out who did it. Just take a look around. Who's missing?" Frank asked.

"Just old Mr. Peters and Fletcher," said Mrs. Ackerly. "But I doubt they'd be able to trudge their way this far into the woods. That old man is much too feeble."

"They're probably listening to birdcalls down by the lake," said her husband.

"I'm not so sure the old man is that old," Randall said suddenly. "I saw him running down a trail once, when he didn't think anybody was around."

"But he's into bird calls," said Joe. "He has a musical chart. We, uh, saw him with it once. It had all the notes, A to H."

"But there is no H note in music," said Mrs. Ackerly.

123

Frank and Joe looked at each other. How could we have missed an important clue like that? both of them were thinking. "It must have been some other kind of chart. It was on thin paper, almost tissue," Joe said.

"Tracing paper!" cried Frank. "Maybe it was an overlay of the lodge map."

"Why would they want that?" asked Mr. Ackerly.

"To find the loot!" Burns blurted out suddenly. Brown and Buckley glanced at him.

"Maybe Fletcher's the fourth member of the gang," Biff suggested. "The one that was never found!"

"You mean Fletcher is actually Ace Birdwell?" Buckley exclaimed. "No way! He died trying to escape through the woods."

"Did he?" Frank said. He turned to Burns. "That was a real person you saw, wasn't it? Not a ghost. A person you recognized. Someone who knew how much you hated and feared the number thirteen."

Burns looked down at the ground. His friends stared straight ahead with no expression on their faces.

"He'd be hard to recognize in a wig and thick glasses, especially if he stayed hunched over all the time," Randall said slowly. "And, of course, we hardly ever noticed him."

"That could explain the early morning ghost," said Brown.

124

"That wasn't one of you?" Joe asked.

The Three B's shook their heads. Then Buckley said, "Look, you know who we are now, but believe me, we didn't cause any of the accidents at the lodge. We didn't even know Peters was really Birdie, until Burns found out."

Frank nodded. "We'll talk to you guys later. You're not totally in the clear yet. One thing's for sure, though. Fletcher and Peters *are* involved."

"But where could they be?" asked Mrs. Ackerly. "Between all of us, we've pretty well covered these woods this morning. Has anyone seen them other than Chet?"

"That must have been the mysterious guy Mike and I saw after we saw the buck," Randall said.

"They're probably at the lodge," Frank said. He turned to Joe. "I think we'd better get back there and have a word with them."

"Chet and I will stay here and keep an eye on the boys from Providence," Biff said. "Alias Jones, Green, and Graham!"

Frank and Joe quickly made their way back to the trail. Fifteen minutes later, they reached the spot where they'd left the ATV.

The brothers piled into the ATV, and Frank started the engine.

"Hold tight, it's going to be a bumpy ride!" Frank shouted as they took off, leaving a cloud of dust behind them.

"We're not breaking any speed records," Joe yelled over the noise of the engine. "But it's faster than walking."

Finally, the Hardys pulled up in front of the lodge. They headed for Peters and Fletcher's cabin.

"Empty," Joe said, after they'd looked around. "They've packed up all their stuff."

"Let's see if they're at the main lodge," said Frank.

The Hardys hurried back to the lodge. They checked the upstairs, living room, and Steve's office. Fletcher and Birdwell were nowhere to be found.

"Let's try the kitchen," Joe said.

They passed through the dining room and pushed open the double doors that led to the kitchen.

Maggie and Sara were seated at one end of the work island in front of a pot of coffee and three mugs. A third person looked up from the other end as the brothers entered the room.

"You remember Captain Jerry Barnes," Maggie said, nodding in the direction of the pilot who had flown them in a few days ago.

"The plane is in?" Joe asked.

"Uh-huh," said Jerry. "Down at the landing dock, as always."

"Are you taking any passengers out today?" Frank asked the pilot.

Captain Barnes shook his head. "No one's booked a flight with me for today."

"What's up?" Sara asked. "Why is everybody in such a hurry today?"

"What do you mean?" Frank asked.

"Nothing. Except, I just saw Mr. Peters and Fletcher rushing on down toward the dock," she replied. "I never thought that old guy could move like that and—"

Frank and Joe didn't wait to hear the rest of her sentence. In a flash they were out of the kitchen and on their way to the dock.

The seaplane was floating in the water against the dock as the waves lapped gently alongside. At first glance, it seemed deserted. But then Frank and Joe saw that part of the engine cover was raised, as though it were being serviced.

Behind the raised cover they found someone dressed like Peters leaning over the engine.

"Well, if it isn't Mr. Peters," said Joe. "Or should I say—*Ace Birdwell.*"

The man lifted his head. He had wispy brown hair and piercing blue eyes. He wasn't wearing thick glasses now.

"So you figured it out." Birdwell smiled menacingly. "You kids must think you're pretty smart."

"We're smart enough to know when the game is up," Joe said angrily. "Your little treasure hunt

127

nearly ruined Steve's lodge—not to mention almost getting us killed a couple of times."

"Why don't you just put down that engine cover and come quietly with us," Frank said.

Birdwell just shook his head. "I don't think so," he said in a clear, strong voice.

Joe took a step toward him. "You're in enough trouble now. Don't make us—"

"Don't move," growled a deep voice from behind them.

The Hardys turned to face the stocky form of Fletcher. He was pointing a .30–.30 rifle right at them.

16 Plane Facts

Frank and Joe stood frozen as Ace Birdwell quickly stepped over to join Fletcher. Now that he had abandoned the stoop he'd used in his Mr. Peters role, Birdwell seemed a good six inches taller, as well as much younger.

"Well, well. Looks like we're going to have a little extra baggage on board for our getaway." Birdwell laughed unpleasantly. "Too bad our little pranks didn't scare you—or the rest of the guests—away."

He took the rifle from Fletcher and covered the Hardys. "Tie them up and gag them," he ordered Fletcher.

Fletcher tackled Joe first, then Frank. After both brothers were bound and gagged, Fletcher carried Joe, then Frank, into the plane.

The Hardys could hear them working under the cockpit hood for a few minutes. Then there was silence, except for the sound of the two men working on the engine.

Moments later Fletcher leaned into the plane. He was smiling with pleasure as he placed a rusty metal box inside the cockpit.

Birdwell quickly swung in the door and got into the pilot's seat. Fletcher went round to the still open engine.

The engine gave a few gasps, then roared to life. Fletcher slammed down the hood, scrambled aboard the plane, and shut his door. Then they were taxiing across the lake.

Over the rush of air and the sound of the propellers, the Hardys could hear Birdwell and Fletcher talking.

"Well, we did it!" Birdwell said. "It took a while to find—we had to clear off all that second growth —but we've got the money now!" He laughed as he piloted the plane into a takeoff. "Weren't you lucky to bump into me up here thirteen years ago?"

"Yeah, but *you* were a lot luckier that I found you in the woods back then," Fletcher said. "You could have frozen to death."

"Right," Birdwell admitted. "The last person I expected to meet when I ducked out of the getaway car was an out-of-work electrical engineer and mechanic, out to do a little illegal hunting. Good thing I didn't turn you in, heh-heh!"

"You weren't in any big hurry to meet the sheriff, the way I remember it," Fletcher told him.

"I might have ended up in jail like those other idiots. I was the brains of that gang, you know. Who do you think planned that big robbery in the first place? And figured out the best place to stash the loot? But they never gave me enough credit. Morons! They couldn't do anything right." Birdwell began laughing again. "But I've fixed them now. No money for them. You and I will share it, once we're out of here."

"Funny how you couldn't remember where you buried it," Fletcher said.

"That's because Jones, Green, and Graham kept digging it up for themselves. It was a nightmare. I had to keep moving it—couldn't trust them. And they didn't trust me. It got to the point that every time I left the lodge, they'd follow me.

"But finally, I took a chance and went out in the middle of a blinding snowstorm," Birdwell continued. "I could hardly see ten feet in front of me, but it was worth it. They didn't follow me that time! I buried the box in a clearing in the woods. It took me a while to find the clearing again after so many years, but I did!"

"And you waited all this time to dig up the money again," Fletcher said.

131

"That's right," Birdwell replied. "I was a wanted man, remember? Until that day I called and asked if you wanted to dig up the money with me, I was holed up in a small town in Canada."

The plane had been climbing steadily. Now it began to level off. Frank craned his neck to try to see out the window. He managed to get a glimpse of water beneath them. Maybe we're flying over Moosehead Lake, he thought. Then he rejected that idea. It was more likely that they were flying north, to Canada.

"But I still don't understand why we have to change our names and everything," the Hardys heard Fletcher say. "Do you really think someone might be able to track us down?"

"There's always some two-bit detective looking to make a name for himself, like these kids back there," Birdwell told him. "And there's no sense in taking any chances. We have to disappear from the face of the earth. Once everyone figures we died along with the loot, it'll all be over." He paused for a moment. Then he said, "You're sure you got this thing figured right?"

"Hey, remember, I was an electrical engineer in the old days," said Fletcher. "Trust me. Now, let's go over it again.

"First, we turn the plane back toward Lakeside Lodge. Then we set the plane on automatic pilot. Once we bail out, it will head straight for the lodge.

Your 'friends' should be back by then and it'll wipe them out at the same time we 'perish.' There won't be a trace."

"No trace at all," Birdwell went on gleefully. You take the inflatable boat and the little electric motor with you. Then I follow with the box of money. Did you change the battery last night?"

"Sure did," Fletcher replied.

"Good," Birdwell said. "Once you pick me up, we'll head across the lake to that spot where you stowed the car, right?"

"Right," Fletcher said. "What about those two back there? Why don't we just dump them in the lake?"

"They'd float to the surface . . . and someone just might figure things out. No, we'll leave them behind on the plane. They'll be two more casualties when it crashes into the lodge and explodes." Birdwell's laugh sent a chill down the Hardys' spines.

Huddled together in the rear of the cockpit, Frank and Joe stared at each other. It looked as though there was nothing they could do.

"I'll turn her around now and take her up a little higher so there'll be plenty of time for our chutes to open," Birdwell said.

He turned the plane to the right. Then he pulled back on the stick, and the plane began to climb. Frank and Joe were thrown backward. They could just catch a glimpse of the sky from the cockpit window.

"Okay, Fletcher, make sure you have everything securely in your grasp," Birdwell ordered. "When I level off, get set to jump."

The Hardys saw the stocky man get out of his seat, a parachute strapped to his back. He opened the door. Birdwell slowed the plane into almost a glide. "Okay, Fletcher, now—jump!"

Fletcher leapt clear of the door. As the plane circled around, the Hardys got a glimpse of his parachute as it opened and drifted down into the lake.

"Now, I just set these controls," Birdwell muttered to himself, "and off I go."

The Hardys could hear the *click, click, click* of buttons being pushed and switches being set. But from where they were, there was no way they could see what was happening up front.

"Okay," said Birdwell. "Everything's in order. Well, boys, you'll only have a few more minutes to suffer. Then you and those miserable creeps I used to be associated with will all be gone. Let's see, yes, twelve-thirty . . . they should all be just sitting down to lunch. I hope they enjoy the surprise dessert!"

He positioned himself to jump against the pilot's chair. The chair swung around to the left and hit Joe, who was in back of it.

Joe fell halfway between the two seats. He looked up at Birdwell, clutching the metal box as he prepared to jump. There was a triumphant look on the robber's face.

Then Ace Birdwell leapt forward into the sky as the plane continued on its perilous course.

With a little more room in back, Frank managed to rub against the interior fittings and loosen his gag.

"Can you see anything up there?" he gasped.

"Num-uh," Joe croaked from behind his gag.

"That doesn't tell me much," Frank complained.

Worming his way forward until he was practically on top of Joe, Frank lifted up his head until he could see out the cockpit window.

For a moment it was all blue skies. Then, the sound of shifting gears was followed by a brief silence. Then came another click, and the plane started to descend.

As they looked ahead of them, the Hardys could see that they were flying over Mirror Lake—and that the plane was headed straight for Lakeside Lodge.

17 With the Greatest of Ease

"We've got to stop this plane," Frank said desperately. "And that means we have to get free somehow. Joe, can you move forward at all?"

Frank struggled to shift his own weight back off his brother. Joe managed to inch a tiny bit more toward the front of the plane. Wedging himself carefully in the pilot's seat, he pushed his way up against the backrest.

"Great!" Frank said encouragingly. Meanwhile, he rolled to his side, rubbing the ropes that tied his hands against the latches and hooks that held the pilot's seat in place.

Suddenly Frank leaned against the backrest control. Joe lurched forward.

"Lift your head!" Frank shouted. "If you can just lean your chin on that stick in front of you, you might be able to disengage it."

Joe kept nodding and squirming until his chin was resting on the cold handle of the stick.

Then, to Frank's amazement, Joe twisted around on the swivel chair and managed to bring his still-bound hands up and around . . . just enough to reach the control panel.

"Way to go!" Frank exclaimed. "Now let's see if we can undo the automatic pilot."

Joe was busily rubbing his gag against the pilot's stick. Finally the gag pulled free and slipped below his chin.

"I've got an idea," he panted. "Let's see if we can turn this baby around."

He looped the now-loosened gag over the end of the pilot's stick. For the next minute or so, by straining his neck back, he managed to use the gag to help pull the stick slightly to one side.

The plane began to veer off course, leveling off, then pulling a tiny bit to the left.

"We should throw our weight toward that side," Frank suggested. "I'll bet Birdwell forgot to take that into account when he set the automatic."

"You're right," Joe agreed.

They bumped the stick as far as they could to the left, watching as the landscape below changed.

137

Joe yanked a little harder on the stick. The plane continued on its course away from its target.

"What now?" he asked.

"We've passed the lodge, and now we're flying in a circle around the lake," Frank said. "If anyone's watching down below, they'll think we're just out for a joyride."

"Oh, great," Joe said. "The big question is— what happens when the joy ride's over?"

"The way I figure it, we'll eventually run out of fuel," said Frank. "Then we'll gradually glide to a stop somewhere."

"That could be rough," Joe said. "What if we come down on top of those tall pines?"

"I don't think we will," said Frank. "The circles are getting smaller. Odds are we'll end up floating on top of the lake."

The plane continued its circle around the lake. After they had passed the lodge three times, the engine started to sputter. The plane began to lose altitude as the engine became weaker and weaker.

Joe pushed the stick forward very slowly. The plane glided lower and lower over the lake. Then it landed with a gentle splash on the water.

The seaplane floated softly on the calm waters of the lake.

"Good work, Joe," Frank said.

"Hey, nothing to it," Joe replied. "I always

wanted to fly a plane with a gag wrapped around my neck!"

Frank looked out the window. They were about fifteen feet from the lodge's dock.

"Here come Steve and Jerry," said Joe, peering out the window.

Across the water, they heard an angry voice shouting from the dock. It sounded like Jerry Barnes's. ". . . didn't even refuel it yet. Only an hour's worth of flying time . . . they could have gone down in the trees! Who would have tried a nutty stunt like that?"

A gust of breeze brought part of Steve Johnson's answer to them. ". . . can't find Fletcher and Peters —or Birdwell, as these guys call him now . . . and the Hardy brothers are missing."

"Well? What are we waiting for? Come on! Let's get out there and see what's going on!" cried Jerry.

The Hardys saw Steve walk to the end of the dock and climb into an outboard. Jerry Barnes stepped into the boat after him.

Moments later, the Hardys heard the buzzing of the outboard engine as it zoomed its way toward them.

Frank and Joe peered out the window and saw the outboard less than five feet from them. Steve cut the engine and the boat moved more slowly toward the plane.

"I'll turn off the engine and we can paddle right up to it," the Hardys heard Steve say.

"Let's come around on the starboard side," said Jerry Barnes. "We're closer to that side."

Frank and Joe waited. Moments later, the door to the pilot's side of the plane opened.

For a second, the two men in the boat stared dumbfounded through the door at the two teenagers in the plane.

"You guys must be crazy, pulling a stunt like this," Jerry Barnes started to yell. "What do you think—"

"Hold it, Jerry," said Steve. "I don't think they stole your plane."

"Then what—?" Jerry began.

"I think they saved it for you," Steve interrupted. "Haven't you noticed their hands and feet?"

"I—" Jerry Barnes really stared at the Hardys now. "They're tied up! What are we waiting for? Let's untie them!"

Steve tied the boat to one of the plane's struts. The two men climbed into the plane to free the Hardy brothers.

While the lodge owner and the pilot worked at untying them, Frank and Joe revealed everything they had learned from Birdwell and Fletcher during the flight. Steve and Jerry already knew that Peters was actually Birdwell—the group from Horn

Point had arrived back at the lodge, and the Three B's had told them their whole story.

After the Hardys were free, the four of them climbed out of the plane into the outboard. Steve started the engine and they headed for the dock.

"I can't believe it," Jerry said. "Those two airplane hijackers . . ."

"Not to mention robbers and would-be murderers," added Steve.

"And kidnappers—let's not forget that," added Joe.

"They're going to get away, free as the birds," Jerry said, pounding his fist against the side of the boat.

"What makes you think that?" Frank asked suddenly.

The others stared at him, but Frank only began to laugh.

"I don't think they're going anywhere!"

18 It's on the Map

Joe, Steve, and Jerry stared at Frank.

"What are you talking about?" Steve Johnson asked. "Birdwell and Fletcher are probably halfway to Canada by now."

"Only if the current is drifting pretty hard upstream," Frank said. "Or maybe they can paddle real well with their hands."

"I thought you said they had an electric motor with them," said Jerry Barnes.

"Right," Joe said, finally catching on to what Frank was saying. "And they charged the battery for it *all night*."

"Only I didn't have the generator on!" Steve exclaimed, his face breaking into a huge grin.

"If they had the controls in the on position when

they hooked up their battery, it probably drained all night, too," said Joe.

Frank turned to the pilot. "Jerry, once you get that plane up again, you'll probably spot them drifting a few miles offshore somewhere. This lake is as calm as a bathtub right now."

Jerry shook his head. "I don't know how soon I can get the plane up. It's out of fuel, and if those guys monkeyed with my engine, I may have to make repairs—and I doubt if I can do much work out here." Suddenly Jerry Barnes began to smile. "But I'll bet they didn't think to mess with my radio. So I can contact the state police and have them send out a boat to pick up those two guys."

"Tell you what," said Steve. "When we get back, I'll ask Willy to bring out some fuel and his toolbox. The two of you should be able to fix the plane."

"What about our friends, the Three B's?" asked Frank. "They haven't tried to make a break for it a second time, have they?"

Steve laughed.

"When they got back to the lodge and told us their story, they went to their rooms and stayed there—with Biff and Chet for company. The B's said they wanted to make *sure* everyone knew they were innocent."

He shook his head. "But it turns out that Len Randall is really a reporter for some scandal sheet.

143

Mallory keeps going around snapping pictures of the Three B's and Randall pesters them with endless questions. Burnsie said he almost wished he were going back to the pen to get away from them!''

They pulled in at the familiar dock and Steve tied up the boat. When they got back to the lodge, Steve and Jerry left to find Willy.

"With any luck, we'll be able to think of a way to get the plane back to the shore," Steve said.

The Hardys headed up the porch steps and into the living room. "Let's find the Three B's," Frank said to his brother. "There're a few questions *we* want to ask them."

"You'll find them in the kitchen," Maggie announced, coming out of the office. Sara was right behind her. "We put them to work chopping vegetables back there. It's the only place Randall won't think of looking for them."

Frank and Joe looked around a little nervously. "Speaking of the ace news hounds, where are they?" Frank asked. "I don't want to find my face on the front page of their scandal sheet, with a headline like 'Trapped on a Crashing UFO and Lives to Tell the Story!' ''

Sara laughed. "I told those two that Burnsie, Brown, and Buckley had gone back out into the woods to try to bag that six-point buck with a makeshift bow and arrow."

144

Maggie chuckled. "And those fools went after them, saying it would make a great story."

"Have you seen Chet and Biff?" Joe asked.

"One of them's gone running—and the other has a Do Not Disturb sign on his door," said Sara.

"I guess we don't have to guess who's doing what," Joe said.

"And I don't suppose you'd tell us what we're having for dinner?" Frank said teasingly.

"You'll find out when everyone else does," Maggie told him flatly. Then she turned around and went back to the kitchen.

The Hardys sat by the warm fire for a while. Then they left the lodge and headed for their cabin to wash up. They had just reached the path, when they heard the noise of an engine out on the lake.

Frank and Joe hurried down to the dock in time to see Jerry Barnes's seaplane taxi across the water. Then it took off.

Willy pulled up at the dock in the outboard. "Jerry got on the radio to the state police," he reported. "They said they'd mount a search for Birdwell and Fletcher right away."

"Good," Joe said. "The sooner those two are locked away the better."

The Hardys walked back to the path that led to their cabin. They cleaned up and headed over to the lodge for dinner. Just as they seated themselves around the table, Len Randall and Mike Mallory came in.

"Just the guys I'm looking for!" Randall exclaimed.

Frank and Joe groaned. They knew it was no use trying to hide from the reporter now.

The Hardys filled Randall and Mallory in on their adventure in the plane.

"But there are still a few things we never found out from those two," Frank said. "Maybe we can get some answers from our friends from Providence."

"Hey, wait a minute, guys," Randall protested. "They've just about promised me an exclusive on their story."

"Look, Randall, we just want the story from them. We're not going to publish it," Frank told him.

"We haven't told you absolutely *everything* Birdwell said or did," Joe added. He frowned. "Of course, if you're not interested . . ."

"Oh, I *am* interested," Randall said eagerly.

"Well, then you just leave the Three B's to us, and we'll get you everything you need," Frank said.

Chet and Biff stepped into the dining room.

"Are you guys okay?" Chet asked Frank and Joe. "Steve told us what happened to you."

"We're fine, Chet," Frank said to his friend.

Biff came over and gave both Hardys walloping

blows on the shoulder. "Glad to see you two made it back in one piece," he said. Then he added, "This place is really wild."

"Much too hectic," Chet agreed, with a yawn.

The Ackerlys strolled into the lounge, smiling as though they had a big secret. Before anyone could say anything, however, Maggie announced that the evening meal was going to be a little late but worth waiting for.

She returned to the kitchen, where she shooed the Three B's out the door.

Looking solemn, Burns, Buckley, and Brown stepped into the dining room. Steve and Willy came in and sat at the table.

"Since we're all here, except Maggie and Sara—" Frank began.

"—who are involved in an important mission," put in Mr. Ackerly.

Frank looked at him in puzzlement, but continued, "—there are a few points we'd like to clear up."

Everyone began talking at once.

Joe blew a sharp whistle blast through his fingers.

"We'll start at the beginning," Frank said. "First, the ghost. Birdwell or Fletcher must have stolen the ATV and careened around in it dressed up as a ghost. Fletcher was a mechanic and electrical engineer, so he knew how to use every piece of equipment at the lodge. Birdwell's old man disguise fooled everyone. No one would suspect an elderly man of causing those 'accidents.'"

"They bugged the phone and must have had a receiver stashed somewhere near their cabin. Fletcher was probably listening in on a call that time Frank and I saw him with that 'personal stereo' on," said Joe.

"And, of course, they rigged up the exploding device—just in case they needed to put the phone out of order," Frank said.

"But why all the fuss? Why didn't they just go, dig up the box, and get out of here?" asked Mr. Ackerly.

"I think we can answer that—since we're technically in the clear," Buckley said. "Birdie probably didn't know for sure where it was. If he could scare everyone away from here, he'd have the whole area all to himself. He wouldn't have to wear that disguise anymore."

He looked around at the other guests. "You see, we never trusted one another. Birdwell buried the loot, but then someone would dig it up and bury it somewhere else. So we kept an eye on one another and kept moving the box around."

"Until Birdwell went out in that blizzard, buried the money, and wasn't heard of until now."

Brown nodded. "After that, none of us knew where the money was hidden," he said. "So we couldn't tell the cops when they caught up with us." He grinned. "While we were doing time, we agreed we'd all go after the money as soon as we got out."

Brown shook his head. "Birdie must have lost a few marbles wandering around in the freezing cold when he made his break for it. He must have heard that we were getting out, and he had to come after the stuff himself."

"With his pal who rescued him," added Joe.

"So that's who Fletcher was," said Burns.

"So all the time, you were just out in the woods looking for the money peacefully?" asked Frank.

The Three B's nodded. "And we really just wanted to see if the money was still here," Buckley said. "We even looked at the map we left in the tool shed years ago, but it didn't help us much."

"We're just three ex-cons living on memories," Brown said with a sigh.

"We just got out of prison," Burns added. "We didn't want a ticket back *in* there!"

"Imagine, being out here all week and no one got anything worth taking a picture of." Mallory sighed.

"I got a story," Randall said happily. "Which do you think is the better headline: 'Cons Hunt Years-Old Loot' or 'Trapped on a Crashing Plane'?"

"I think the money angle is the way to go," Frank said, rolling his eyes.

"Which reminds me, you'll have to thank us for dinner, won't they, Arthur," said Mrs. Ackerly.

"You mean, you got a deer?" Chet asked weakly.

"Oh, no," she said. "I thought that airplane buzzing over the lake might stir things up. So we found a charming little cove this afternoon and went angling. We're having trout for dinner."

"Fishing! Now that's something we could do tomorrow, Frank," Joe said enthusiastically. "I can see the headline now," he added with a grin. " 'Teen Detectives Net Fishy Catch.' "

"Instead of 'Get Caught in a Fishy Net'?" Frank asked with a smile. The brothers looked at each other and burst out laughing.

THE HARDY BOYS® SERIES By Franklin W. Dixon